THRILLING ADVENTURES 2

RUSS CROSSLEY

53RD STREET PUBLISHING

EXCERPT

Artificial intelligences can be so difficult when they want to be.

RED activated the rocket pack's maneuvering jets to move them far enough away from the door so the blast wouldn't affect them then triggered the weapon. The bomb blew the door in accompanied by a shower of sparks and a loud thump audible over then the wind. Acrid smoke billowed out from the passenger cabin swept away by the force of the rushing air at this altitude. The twin external rocket engines on the dirigible were still running and Red could register the heat. They needed to avoid going near the exhaust ports of the powerful engines.

"Hold on. We're going in fast. Prepare to fire at any moving target."

"Okay, RED." Virtue responded his tone sharp and focused.

A hint of doubt occurred to RED suggested by previous experience. "Set your weapon on stun, Virtue, we don't need another Toledo." He didn't respond but she knew he understood. The last thing they needed were multiple fatalities as they did in that dead end bar outside the Ohio city when Virtue in a panic fired his weapon into a crowd of angry bikers.

THRILLING ADVENTURES 2

Edited by R. Edgewood

53RD STREET PUBLISHING

Published by 53rd Street Publishing
Offices in Gibsons, B.C. Canada and Lincoln City, Oregon

OTHER COLLECTIONS AND ANTHOLOGIES FROM THE AUTHORS

Tales of Urban Fantasy
Tales of Bizarre Detectives
Tales of Mystery and Suspense
Tales of Weird Fantasy
Tales of Twisted Crime
Tales of The Unexpected
Tales From Space
10 by Russ Crossley
Round Up At The Burger Bar: The Story of Trixie Pug,
Parts 1- 5 The Beginning
Worlds of Science Fiction and Fantasy
More Tales of Mystery and Suspense
Justice Served
Love Stories
Ladies of the Jolly Roger
The Adventures of Razor and Edge:
An Unexpected Journey
On Edge
Thrilling Adventures

Total War
Ten Tempting Tales with R.S. Meger
The Fantastic Five with R.S. Meger
Unique Tales of the Fantastic
Tales of the Fantastic

ACKNOWLEDGMENTS

To the intrepid astronauts who inspired many of the following generations to reach for the stars and other places of our collective imaginations. Thank you.

DEDICATION

For all those who share my love of the fantastic.

Thrilling Adventures 2

Edited by R. Edgewood

Published by 53rd Street Publishing

Cover art ©grandfailure
Cover designed by R. Edgewood
Cover design and layout © 2019 by 53rd Street Publishing

Print ISBN: 978-1-927621-67-7

53rd Street Publishing
Head office: Gibsons B.C. Canada
www.53rdstreetpublishing.com

INTRODUCTION

In this second volume of Thrilling Adventures you will find selected works by two of our talented authors. The stories selected for this volume are very exciting reads and stretch our—and hopefully you, the readers—imaginations to the limit.

We truly hope you enjoy these tales and will seek out other works by these wonderful writers.

R. Edgewood
July 2019

TABLE OF CONTENTS

SCAVENGERS

Russ Crossley

Tey Wilks stole a peek over the jagged rocks of the sun dried moss covered, partially collapsed, stonewall over looking the vast rows of shabby one hundred and sixty story buildings running away from the hill he was on as far as the horizon. The odors of rotting garbage, mold, and stale cooking smells wafted over him carried by the constant breeze, but didn't penetrate his consciousness. He had grown up around the cesspools of this city of over a five hundred million residents so his senses were numb to such an odiferous atmosphere. In all his long life he had never once been outside city limits so the massive city was all he knew. He swept the strands of his shoulder length chestnut brown hair away from his face.

He then dropped back down behind the wall fearful a marauder gang might spot him. Marauder gangs conducted sweeps looking for citizens weakened by hunger unable to defend themselves, or the injured, or those suffering from disease.

The government paid the gangs a bounty for each citizen they captured, but there were rumors the gangs would take any citizen they caught outside their homes after twilight.

Since the atmosphere had grown thick with pollutants twilight was now a moveable target depending on the weather. If it rained heavy enough to knock down the pollutants in the air twilight could be delayed. Of course given the infrequency of rainfall twilight conditions had grown longer and longer in recent years. Soon the smog would be so thick twilight would own the daylight hours. Consequently with each passing year the marauder gangs had become bolder.

The rumors said those citizens too weak from hunger, and those suffering debilitating injuries, were executed at government facilities. The rumor also said a team of immunologists assessed the diseased. Citizens with a communicable disease were isolated for experimental purposes.

This is where the substantiated rumors stopped. No one knew what these experiments were meant to determine, or what happened to the citizens after the experiments were complete. This is where the wild speculation and conspiracy theories sprouted like mushrooms in a damp basement.

Tey's favorite of these crazy theories said once diseases were isolated they were tested on cities and that millions died in agony. But since communication between cities was spotty this had never been confirmed. No one he knew, or ever heard of, had died from illness or natural causes in over a hundred years. The government wasn't about to reveal what they were doing to the citizenry. They controlled every aspect of life on the planet.

Moving away from the wall crouching low to shield himself from anyone looking in his direction he quickly came to the end of the sun browned brown grassy area behind the wall. Tey's mission was to scavenge for food, bottles of fresh water, and other supplies needed by his pod of apartments.

A pod consisted of six apartments occupied by one hundred and forty-eight people. He was one of sixteen volunteer scavengers from his pod scouring the city for the ever more precious supplies. Competing scavengers were as big a threat as the marauders hence Tey was armed with two pistols, and four knives of varying lengths, hidden about his ragged, soiled clothes. He would kill if necessary.

The survival of his pod, and him, depended on acquiring the necessary quota of supplies. No one was about to stand in his way and live if they tried to prevent him form reaching his quota as far as he was concerned. If he failed to meet his quota too often his pod mates would break his legs and leave him outside for the next marauder sweep. He'd seen it done many times in his seventy-two years.

He froze, sucking in his breath, and his heart began to beat rapidly when something to his right made a cracking sound. He hoped it was a competitor and not a marauder gang. Peering into the growing darkness he was a little relieved to see a single figure shrouded in shadow move near the deserted warehouse across the field from him. He would have stood very little chance of surviving if this was a marauder gang.

Swallowing hard he scurried to his right hoping to flank the potential threat. Muffled footsteps came from somewhere to his left.

Tey fell on his belly in the dry grass and pulled one of his pistols from its holster. He held it out aiming into the darkness. His own rapid breathing echoed in his head.

There was a flash suppressor affixed the barrel of his gun so even if he missed the target wouldn't be able to see where the shot came from. His eyes had adjusted to the darkness so he could see a human shaped silhouette standing near the opening where the door used to be to enter the warehouse.

After taking careful aim he shouted for the person to freeze and drop their weapon. The shadow dropped to the ground and a burst of gunfire, accompanied by brilliant muzzle flashes, sent a barrage of bullets whizzing over his head. Tey fired back, three successive shots aimed at the source of the flashes followed by a satisfying cry of pain, then stillness.

Tey waited straining to hear any sounds from the target. After several minutes the tension in his body eased and he stood and began to move toward the warehouse keeping his gun at the ready just in case. Finally he stood over the body and realized his shots had been more accurate than he hoped. The woman, dressed in a head-to-toe one-piece black jumpsuit, lay on her back her dead gaze staring up at him. Holstering his own gun he knelt beside her and quickly found her gun and two knives, which he stuffed into his belt. It didn't appear she'd managed to scavenge any supplies, which was too bad. It would have made his job easier to steal what he needed from a corpse, at least for today.

Realizing the brief firefight would attract unwanted attention he hurried away until he was once again swallowed by the darkness. Soon he was following an old dirt road into an area of the city he had never been before. He'd been tracking a government caravan for several days hoping the vehicles had plenty of food and other supplies he could poach from without being noticed. The tracks of the convoy of trucks left deep ruts in the roads so they were carrying something heavy. Very heavy given the depth of the tire tracks.

That woman he just killed must have been on the same mission as him, which meant there were probably other scavengers around. He had to be careful.

As he walked over a slight rise in road he saw lights coming from a massive warehouse about a mile away. He estimated the building was several acres in size and could easily swallow a fleet of trucks. Scanning the terrain visible between him and the warehouse he couldn't make out a lot of details in this darkness, but what he could make out caused him concern. There wasn't a lot of cover to hide his approach.

A marauder gang, or the security force no doubt guarding the convoy, would take him out long before he reached the objective.

Considering his options for several seconds he decided to try the direct approach and see how good the security truly was. He walked in the middle of the road until he came to a wire fence. Along the top of the fence were closed circuit cameras that swiveled to cover the length of the fencing both east and west of the gate. The heavy steel pad lock affixed to the gate prevented him from easy access. But there were no guards, armed or otherwise, standing at or near the entrance to the warehouse. The doors were closed so he couldn't see the interior but a row of small windows approximately five feet from the roof line ran the length the building. Golden rays of light were visible through the windows. They appeared to fluctuate rather than provide steady illumination. He wondered what that meant.

The smell of mud and grass permeated Tey's senses...it suddenly dawned on him the grass didn't smell sun burned as it did everywhere else in the city. How was this possible? His eyes narrowed as he studied the warehouse and surrounding area in front of the warehouse doors. There was something odd about this building. But what?

His eyes went wide. It isn't old.

The fence, the cameras, the warehouse itself were all newer than anything he had ever seen. As the population density increased dramatically beginning seventy years ago all construction stopped when every available building sites were occupied. Almost every continent contained massive cities with multibillions of citizens. One world government maintained strict control of food and water supplies and other daily necessities after the world wide financial system collapsed decades ago.

"Don't move," said a stern male voice behind him. Tey froze

where he stood and closed his eyes expecting to be shot at any second. "Check him," said the voice.

A rough pair of hands pushed Tey face first into the fence and began to search him. Soon his guns and knifes, and those he stole off the dead scavenger, were on the ground around him. "Okay, step back. No sudden moves." Tey did as instructed and waited as two hushed voices, one male, the other female, discussed in rapid fire tones something for a minute or two. Finally the female voice instructed him to turn around.

When Tey did he found himself facing two scavengers he knew. Malt and Ergo from zone 5567.2. The three of them cooperated on a successful mission a few years back. Between them they split a massive haul that provided supplies for their respective apartments for five weeks.

"You two interested in a pact?" Tey said.

Malt and Ergo exchanged looks of distain in their hazel eyes. The shorter, pale blond Ergo pulled her pistol from her holster. "Hold on." Tey raised his hands. "Listen, I've been following this convoy for weeks and it is the largest concentration of supplies I have ever seen. Far larger than the last time we worked together."

Ergo briefly shifted her gaze to Malt. "Some of the food we stole last time was rotten within a week. Ours lost two babies," Malt growled, running a thick hand through his thin gray hair. The jagged scar running down his left cheek paled as he spoke.

"I'm very sorry, but there was no way to know. Some of our food was spoiled too." He nodded toward the warehouse. "This warehouse is newly constructed. Something strange is going on here. Something we should all profit from."

"Why should we trust you?" Ergo spat the words. She took a step closer to Tey raising the gun to waist height as she did so.

"I witnessed soldiers loading boxes in the back of one of the trucks at one of their stops."

Malt arched an eyebrow at him. "So what?"

"I'll kill 'em," said Ergo a slow grin spreading across her lips as her humorless eyes narrowed. "And I'll enjoy it."

"The boxes were labeled emergency supplies."

Malt froze and his eyes widened. "Hold on, Ergo. He may be onto something."

Ergo scowled at her partner. She obviously really wanted to kill Tey. With a grunt of distain she holstered her weapon and stepped back beside her partner. She crossed her arms over her chest and scowled at Tey.

"What do you think was in those boxes?" asked Malt.

Tey shrugged. "I don't know exactly but when they had the back of the truck open for loading it was packed top to bottom with boxes. And the convoy was at least fifty trucks." A sardonic smile spread across Tey's square jawed features. "That's a lot of emergency supplies."

"Why do we need you?" asked Ergo sarcastically.

"Because I'm stupid enough to be the bait to get us inside." He nodded toward the warehouse behind them.

Malt grinned and nodded. He understood.

———

Tey glanced over his left shoulder and peered into the darkness. He knew Malt and Ergo were close by but he couldn't see them. They had the managed to sneak up on him undetected so it wasn't surprising they were invisible to what he was about to do. It did feel good he had his weapons hidden on his body again, but it was unlikely he'd get the use them as he wanted to.

Swallowing hard he approached the massive padlock. He pulled out a pistol and fired a single shot at the lock. The bullet made a sharp ping as it ricocheted off the heavy gauge steel without breaking the lock. An ear splitting siren erupted in the quiet startling him with three short blasts then went silent once again.

He put away his pistol and waited with his arms hanging loose at his sides. No sense in drawing unnecessary fire.

Three heavily armed soldiers appeared through the warehouse door. They wore head-to-toe body armor, Kevlar helmets, and hefted large caliber automatic rifles.

"Freeze," one of them shouted at him. The three soldiers fanned out two acting as guards training their weapons to the left and right of the solider who had shouted at Tey and was now pointing his weapon at him. Tey could imagine what would have happened if he'd actually destroyed the lock however unlikely. I would have extra holes in my body.

"Hands up," instructed the solider aiming his weapon at him. Tey did as he was told keeping his eyes on the solider doing the talking.

"Any sign of others?" The two guards shouted the all clear but kept their weapons at the ready. "Mills, pop the lock." The large man to the left of Tey assumed was the leader slung his weapon around his body and pulled out a small black device form his pocket. He pressed a button on the device and the pad lock disengaged. "Open the gate."

Mills removed the padlock and swung the gate inward while the other guard remained a few paces away continuing to scan the area with the weapon.

Once outside they surrounded Tey and the one in command stepped close to Tey. "Name?"

"Tey Wilks, Sir."

"You military?" Tey shook his head. "Then don't call me Sir. My name is Ruse. I'm in command. And you, buddy, are an intruder on government property."

"I'm with a marauder gang," explained Tey.

Ruse lifted his goggles covering his eyes and arched at

eyebrow at Tey then looked him up and down. "Is that so?" He thought about Tey's explanation for several seconds before continuing. "Why are you alone? Marauders always operate in gangs."

Tey nodded. "My gang was ambushed by a group of scavengers...I was the only survivor. I've come here to get help. They could be close by."

Tey watched the three soldiers tense just as he hoped. Two of them started to walk away from the gate also just as he'd hoped their backs to him and Ruse. Suddenly there were two soft thumps and the two soldiers dropped to the ground. Ruse began pulling his side arm from the holster on his belt, but Tey stepped forward before Ruse had it fully out of the holster and punched the man in the center of his chest as hard as he could. Ruse was still off balance so he fell backward landing hard on his back. A third thump and Ruse slumped back and lay still. Tey saw a dart sticking from the man's arm.

"Hey, why didn't you just shoot these guys?" Tey said to Malt when he appeared from the darkness.

"The military gets very pissed with scavengers who kill soldiers and we don't need the heat." Malt kicked at one of Ruse's boots to make sure he wasn't playing possum. When Ruse didn't move he grunted. "Fast acting," he added anticipating Tey's next question. "They'll be out for hours. Provided the warehouse isn't littered with these types we should have plenty of time to pick over the contents of those boxes." He glanced at Ergo who had joined them from where she'd been hiding.

"I know how to hotwire their trucks," Tey offered, hoping it was enough not to get shot now that they were inside. They needed to see his continued living had some benefit for them, especially as they feel the rotten supplies from their last joint venture were his fault.

Ergo frowned. "What kind of trucks are they?"

"Army issue. Probably those Mack models they favor. Usually

a hybrid engine these days. I figure it burns used cooking oils and electric." Tey watched Ergo's uncertain gaze shift to Malt who cursed under his breath. She was the hotwire expert, but she'd never hotwired military vehicles. They'd need these trucks to move this quantity of supplies. Tey had just had his survival card punched, at least until the trucks were ready to roll. He needed to negotiate the rest of the way.

"Listen, Malt, I'm thinking we should bring the trucks out together because it will be a much larger haul than two trucks. I'd be willing to split half my share between you two if my safety is assured."

Malt's eyes shifted briefly to his partner. Her had become mouth a thin line. She didn't want to make the deal. She was eager to kill him. A little too eager from Tey's perspective.

Malt shook his head and grinned at Tey. "Good play." He shrugged. "Sure, why not. Besides we can use the help loading the stuff." He eyed Ergo. "Stand down. Three pairs of hands make the work go quickly and the haul larger."

Ergo avoided his gaze. "Yeah. Okay," she whispered gruffly before she swung her rifle attached to a sling behind her back.

"Let's adjourn this for now and see what if anything we discover in the warehouse," Malt said, nodding toward the massive structure behind them. They nodded in unison.

Once inside with their pistols out ready for any opposition they discovered rows upon rows of steel shelving stacked high with boxes, the words EMERGENCY SUPPLIES emblazoned across them, running down the right side of the massive facility as far as they were able to see. On the left side of the warehouse was parked a fleet of military trucks identical to the ones he'd seen loading when he first started on this journey.

Tey's heart nearly leapt out of his chest with excitement at the sight. There was no way he had any idea the potential haul would be this big. If he'd known he would have brought the entire scavenger team from his pod with him. Even then they would only made a dent in a load this big, which was a double-edged sword in the scavenger game.

Hauling away all they could carry would hopefully not attract too much attention. The military expected some leakage, as they called it. Small losses were tolerated, large ones were unforgiveable and forced serious retribution with heavy weapons. No pod would ever permit their scavengers to attract such attention if they wanted to remain among the living. Though at times Tey wouldn't call their day-to-day survival living.

Malt ran up to one of the shelving units and began to open one of the boxes. Ergo joined him and together they dragged the box from the shelf onto the warehouse floor. The echo of their footsteps and their excited but hushed tones echoed off the far away walls and the vastness of this place. Tey sniffed the air and was assaulted by a strong odor of machine oil. Something seemed wrong, but he couldn't quite tell what. It was as if there was a word just on the tip of his tongue he couldn't remember.

Malt froze when the box was open. He stared inside wide-eyed as if stunned by his discovery. Ergo cursed under her breath. Tey joined them and immediately saw what had caused such reactions after the initial excitement.

The box was filled with glass jars much like the old canning jars he'd pilfered in his early days of scavenging. Inside the jars were sealed glass tubes filled with purplish liquid.

"What the hell is this?" said Malt rising to his feet his features twisted in rage. He glared at Tey his hands curled into fists.

Suddenly the sounds of leather boots running and the click of safeties being disengaged filled the vast warehouse. "Don't move," said a deep male voice behind them.

A sharp, sudden pain struck the middle of his back. It made him start with surprise and he sucked a breath in. Quickly his mind whirled and darkness closed in until the world disappeared into blackness.

———

"End program."

The scene of the warehouse disappeared and with it the soldiers, and the scavengers, Malt and Ergo and Tey. All that remained was an empty chamber with reflective walls and a matching floor.

"So, Mr. Wilks, what is this simulation program of yours supposed to prove?" said a bald man in a dark suit, white shirt, and a red power tie. His blue eyes were focused on the slim, wiry man across the table from him with granny glasses covering his brown eyes grasping a data pad in his hands. In contrast to the man seated at the table he was dressed in faded corduroy pants, worn sneakers, and a brown-and-yellow checkered shirt with no tie. His mouse brown hair was slicked back on his narrow head.

"Well, Sir, we have run this simulation one hundred and forty seven times and the most common outcome is that in approximately a hundred years from now the world will end."

The man seated at the table arched both eyebrows. "I'm not sure I understand."

"In the next hundred years with medical advances life extension drugs will increase life spans around the planet upwards of more than one hundred and fifty years. At the same time climate change will force the production of GMO foods in underground facilities adapted for darker conditions with no natural sunlight. Pollution and environmental changes will scour the Earth of most animal life and vegetation. The oceans will be drained and desalinated to create drinking water for the estimated fifty billion people on the planet."

"Okay, so we survive," said the man raising his hands palms

up above the table. "That's good news. Not the end of the world as you so dramatically put it." He rose from the chair and smoothed his expensive suit with the palms of his hands.

"But, Sir, you don't understand. Once all our resources are exhausted the world will end."

The man in the suit arched an eyebrow at Wilks and glared at him. "How?"

"The simulation we created extrapolates the vials in those glass jars in the warehouse in this version of the program contain a toxin designed to be powerful enough to kill ninety five percent of the human race in one day."

The man snorted derisively and shook his head as he closed the buttons on his suit jacket with his long tapered fingers. "You think the government is going to wipe out ninety five percent of the human race?" He grinned to himself. "Scavengers. Marauder gangs. Cities with billions of people. Tranquilizer darts. Science fiction," he muttered dismissively under his breath.

Tey Wilks shook his head his expression grim. "No. I do not. My simulations prove the toxin will kill every human and animal on the planet. Even microscopic life will perish. My tests confirm the formulation will be slightly off, just enough to allow it to mutate and wipe out all life on Earth."

The man chuckled. "Of course." He started to walk to the exit door. "I'll take your recommendations to the National Science Council and they will take them to the President and the United Nations Security Council. I assure you this simulation will receive the highest priority it deserves." He opened the door and the last Tey saw of him was the door slamming shut behind him.

"I'm sure it will," Tey whispered in the now quiet holo lab. They were all doomed.

DARK NIGHT

Rita Schulz

P rincess Kora Nicole Sinclair stood on the hard gray cement balcony of her penthouse apartment looking out over the black, cold water of False Creek. The sky was heavy with dense dark clouds.

She wondered what it would be like if she could launch herself from here and fly. Just open her arms fall then soar up into the black of night.

The breeze was crisp even for her, for most humans it would have been bone chillingly cold in the sleeveless sheer black crepe, ankle length dress she wore, but she hardly felt it. Her straight shoulder length honey blonde hair swirled around her face and shoulders almost masking her dark flat ebony eyes. Being a hybrid human and vampire had its advantages at times.

On her left were the lights of the Science Center—or as Vancouverites called it the Golf Ball—and before her twinkled a few street lights and boats bobbing in False Creek on this cold

January evening. To her right were the viaduct and the lights of downtown Vancouver.

Kora knew she should feel cold, but didn't, but she did feel Helen, her trusted aid, secretary and finance officer as she slipped a warm burgundy fur wrap around Kora's shoulders.

Kora was bored this evening. Despite being a world-class detective she hadn't had a good case in months. She needed a diversion. The boredom at her age, a very young looking three hundred, was weighing on her. She knew she had to make a decision, to have children or not. Her mother had contacted her again to tell her once again it was now in the next five years, or never.

Kora lifted her head as she heard Karl, the building manager's two German shepherds, howling below them. Just then her cell phone pinged as the computer started doing its email notification chime.

Someone was trying to get hold of her.

"Thank you, Helen," she said turning her attention to the tall, blonde lovely Helen who was wearing a dark blue fleece shirt and pants. The blue accented her blonde hair and blue eyes.

"You're welcome, Princess," said Helen with a slight smile on her lips.

"Really, Helen, not between the two of us."

"Princess, as you know here on a balcony especially over water sound travels very well." Helen spoke softly so only Kora's sensitive hearing would be able to catch the words.

"And that's one of the reasons we put evergreen trees in large planters on the deck and even native sword ferns in hanging baskets from the railing around the deck too. It helps with the sounds as well as the look, remember how sterile the deck looked?"

"Yes. I better go in and see who wants me and for what. It's a new moon and there is something in the air. Do you feel it?" asked

Kora as she turned to go through the expansive glass balcony doors.

Helen gently sniffed the air tilting her head slightly to listen intently to the dogs below. She looked at Kora and smiled. "Good, you've been bored for too long. Maybe it's time to go hunting again," she said as she waited for Kora to walk past her into the living room.

The apartment was large and contained three bedrooms all of generous proportions and three luxurious bathrooms. The living and dining room had light maple hardwood floors and were open but at the same time intimate. The dining room had a vintage teak dining table that opened up to seat twelve people with a double-sided fireplace so the fire could be seen from both the dining area and the living room.

The walls were painted a soft gray-brown that accented the sea foam and cream couches and chairs. There were large dramatic paintings on the walls helping to separate the living areas and giving them energy as well as potted trees creating cozy conversation areas. Even large delicate ferns and orchids of different colors lent to the feeling of living, growing that brought the outside in.

Helen shivered as she slipped off Kora's fur wrap and put it into the hall closet. Kora went into the study to check the computer and her cell phone.

An email message, marked urgent carried the family seal and crest. She scanned it quickly automatically committing everything to memory. Another perk of her vampire heritage.

"Grandmother has gone missing," Kora said somberly. "She has to be recovered and delivered in time for the meeting the Five Hundred meeting on Monday. She's not just chairing it she also has a few critical items to bring forward." Kora headed into her bedroom walk-in-closet.

Kora quickly contacted Reinhold, her mother's valet and

manservant. If anyone knew where grandmother was he would. Then she quickly contacted the rest of the immediate family for any news of updates on the grand-dame.

The Vampire Consortium was hiring her to find and return their leader, Catherine Sinclair, her grandmother, to make sure she was at the five year meeting of the Five Hundred the world ruling houses which was going to be in Switzerland this year, on January 15th.

There wasn't much time to find her grandmother. But something was strange, it didn't quite feel like a normal kidnapping. Besides how in the world did someone manage to kidnap a mature, vampire with all her guards and soldiers from her home castle?

"Helen, do you know where Robert is? I need him now. We'll be leaving in fifteen minutes and will be gone for maximum five days." Helen pulled down a small hand-carry soft-sided light gray suitcase from the shelf and threw it onto her bed.

"I think he may be in our garage, I'll text him and let him know your plans. Will you need the car and the jet?" asked Helen as she scooped up the black dress Kora discarded on the floor followed by her bra and panties.

"I would like him to accompany me. Yes, we'll need the car and the jet. We'll be going to Grandmother's house in Berlin and then to Switzerland for the meeting." Kora watched Helen text on her own cell phone.

"Will you be needing me during that time?" asked a soft voice from the hallway. Gail her newest employee, a tall slender red haired girl of about twenty-nine, standing waiting for her instructions from Kora.

"Actually Gail, I think I'd like to leave you here to check on any messages that might come in and also take care of any deliveries too," instructed Kora. It was time to increase Gail's responsibilities.

Gail smiled and nodded. She knew Kora would let her know what she would need to do her job well.

Kora was very pleased with Helen and Robert they had been in her employees for a good twenty years and she trusted them implicitly.

Kora and Helen spoke in clipped abbreviated sentences as they quickly got Kora dressed and packed. Helen stood back and looked at Kora. She was wearing black wool pants and a silk shirt with a deep burgundy light hip length light jacket and over that she had a half-the- way down the thigh length over coat.

Kora looked at Helen with a quizzical expression on her face. They hadn't heard from Robert yet. That was completely unheard of he was always ready in less than five minutes.

Kora slipped on her flat walking shoes, grabbed her case and headed for the apartment door. She heard a soft russell behind her and knew Helen had grabbed her travel case, slipped on her walking shoes and her over coat.

"Helen, you stay here. I'll go to the car park to check on Robert and contact you." Kora opened the hall door, looked both ways, and listened for anything that didn't seem normal.

She heard soft steps behind her and knew it was Helen. "Helen, I told you to stay in the apartment," Kora said in a stern clipped voice.

"I heard you say something, Princess, but couldn't quite make out all of your words and decided it was best to come with you and protect your back in case something has happened to Robert." Helen spoke calmly as she strode close to but a little behind Kora.

Kora remember a very long time ago when she was just coming into her own, she had made her decision to enhance her human existence and accepted the gift of becoming part vampire from her grandmother, a well known biochemical engineer, who then turned her into a hybrid.

Helen was with her then, she sat beside her when needed and

locked Kora in a safe place when needed too. Helen was her shield when she was vulnerable.

Helen was also the one the brought Robert to her five years later and it had been the three of them since then. Kora had settled on being a detective given her skills and interests while Helen took care of Stellar Enterprises Ltd., a lucrative international company with many different subsidiaries and her secretary. Robert was the butler, driver, guard as well as an excellent chef.

Kora would let Helen accompany her at least until they found Robert, Helen's husband of ten years, then Kora would make a decision if Helen would accompany her to retrieve grandmother.

Energy surged through Kora's body at the thought of a dangerous hunt. She ran her tongue along her upper canine teeth and smiled as she felt her long, sharp fangs. She took a deep breath and loosened her hands from the fists. Her fingernails were changing into sharp, hard talons. She didn't wouldn't hurt herself.

It was good to feel fit and ready to fight.

"There is a safe room in the garage," said Kora talking to herself and looking around hoping that she would see something that they missed.

Kora heard the swish of their clothing as they jogged down the carpeted hallway to the stairwell exit. She looked over at Helen to see if she was keeping up or was stressing.

Helen smiled at her and nodded she was okay. Kora collapsed the handle of her suitcase and grabbed it by the handle. Helen did too, making their progress faster and quieter.

They almost flew down the fifteen flights of stairs, something that the stories said that Kora as a vampire should be able to do, but they those were only stories. Kora often wondered what it would be like to launch herself into the air and fly.

Once they reached ground level they continued down the

three parking levels to where Kora had her private large garage and storage rooms.

As they entered the garage Kora held up her fist and they both stopped. Helen held her breath so that Kora could use her sensitive hearing to determine if something was out of the ordinary.

Kora listened and used her senses to determine if there was anyone else there. She was hoping Robert was here somewhere. Nothing moved, nothing breathed.

A lump of tension grew in her stomach. She had depended on Robert for years to cover her back and be her wise council.

She looked at Helen. "Safe room?"

Kora glanced at the solid steel door and saw that the green light was on, which meant it hadn't been activated. She shook her head.

Helen pursed her lips giving a tight nod. She would hold herself together until she knew that Robert was all right or dead. If he were dead she would mourn him privately.

Kora moved into the garage and Helen took the opposite side and they did a quick sweep to make sure that Robert wasn't there. He wasn't but Kora caught a strange smell. A gentle whiff of a perfume, Opium, filled her senses. Interesting, it was a scent that wasn't worn very much anymore. But it was her cousin Irene's favorite, it had become a compulsion, she couldn't help but put a tiny dot on her pulse points everyday.

Why would Irene be here? And where was Robert?

"I'm going to check the trunk of your black Rolls," said Helen as she moved to the large heavy car.

It had been specially made for the princess with bulletproof glass and side panels. Not something Kora liked to drive unless the function or ceremony called for it and then only with an experienced driver.

Kora, watched as Helen stood at the back and clicked the key fob to open up the trunk. She heard Helen scream and was next to her in less than a heart beat.

There was Robert. He was bound, gagged, and very dead. There was no heartbeat that Kora could hear, in fact she could tell that the body was already cooling down. A large heavy lump formed in her chest and her stomach rolled over with acid and bile.

Kora screamed silently in her head as her grief turned into anger. Red-hot fire filled her veins as her eyes turned into a black hole where no light escaped. Whoever did this, for whatever reasons would not escape her revenge.

No matter what the reason, they had taken one of her own, and they would pay with their lives and the lives of their family.

Her mouth was dry when she tried to swallow. She really cared for this man. They had been together for a long time and through a lot of interesting situations.

Kora watched as Helen reached down and stroked Roberts's cheek, her eyes full of tears that were starting to stream down her pale cheeks.

"Is he..." said Helen softly.

Kora was ready to reply when she suddenly heard a soft, thready heartbeat. She waited a moment listening intently then moved past Helen to ripped off the gag and removed the duct tape the bound Robert's arms and legs.

The heartbeat grew stronger as they both watched Robert get more and more color in his face. He slowly opened his eyes and looked at them, his brows wrinkled with uncertainty.

"What..." he asked with a hoarse voice.

"Helen, why don't you get Robert some water," Kora instructed.

Helen got into the Rolls and pulled out some cool water from the small drinks area and brought it to the back of the car. Robert was already sitting up by the time she got back. He took the bottle from her and then took a long pull. He first swished the water in his mouth then swallowed it.

"Princess, I regret I was delayed in bringing round the Rolls," said Robert as he started to swing his legs out of the trunk.

Kora softly shook her head. Robert was always a gentleman and she was his number one priority.

"What happened?" asked Kora.

"I was working in the garage making sure that your fleet of cars are always ready for you. I received the text from Helen that you wanted to leave in fifteen minutes," said Robert as he stood up, brushed off his trousers and pulled down his jacket.

He continued. "I went to my locker to retrieve my carry-on case and heard a noise. As I turned I saw someone, actually three someone's, then everything went black. I just woke up now to discover both of you here, so I assume it's been longer than my customary ten minutes. Correct?"

Helen smiled at Kora the tears in Helen's eyes were now tears of joy. Robert was himself again, a very good thing.

Kora and Helen got into the Rolls with Kora in the drivers seat and Helen in the back. Robert stood next to the driver's door waiting for Kora to move, but she grinned at him. "Robert, today I get to drive you and Helen. It's been along time but my driving will give you some time to recover. All three of us will go to Berlin, to the castle. We need to gather information and my ancient home base is the best place to start."

Kora handed her brief case with her laptop and cell to Helen in the back seat as Robert made his was around the car and sat in the back seat too. "Helen please monitor and organize the information coming in. I've got questions out to the entire family and expect to hear from them soon."

Kora turned on the powerful car as they got in and then they were off through the garage gate and up onto Pacific Boulevard heading to Vancouver International Airport's private plane area.

Because of Kora's sharp hearing she thought she could hear something, a click or a tick, coming from underneath the car. It was very low frequency. Her mind went over the possibilities and only one fit, a bomb.

"Helen, grab my cell phone and both of you get out now!" Kora ordered.

The back seat belts disengaged, the warning alarm sounded on the dashboard, doors open and a thud as two bodies hit and roll on the pavement.

Kora drove the Rolls through the sixteen-foot high metal wire fence that led into an empty lot the city leased out for large artistic performances a short way away.

Once she got into the empty lot she aimed the car toward the dark water hoping it would reach the water before the bomb she was certain was under them exploded.

Then it was her turn. She unlocked her seat belt, opened her door, Rolled out onto pavement.

Whoever it was that captured Robert, it may have been to kill him later, but now she was certain she was the intended target. Whoever they were had broken into the garage to disable Robert and plant a bomb under the Rolls. She'll have to alert the Vancouver bomb squad to make sure they checked her other vehicles.

There was a lot more going on here than a simple kidnapping.

Kora lay on the hard cold asphalt for a moment as different scenarios went through her mind one after the other trying to decide what their next course of action should be.

She stood up and looked around her at the black asphalt, weeds that were doing well in the cracks of the parking lot and the cold dark water in front of her. Suddenly the sky opened up and the heavy icy rain that was promised last night started to drenched them.

Kora heard two sets of running footsteps coming to her from

behind. Still no bomb. The Rolls hadn't quite made it to the water, but was a good way away from any apartments in the area.

"Helen, don't call..." There was no other sound except the rolling blast of intense sound and heat coming from the Rolls as it burst into flames and rolled into the water.

Everything was quiet, and then slowly the normal noises of a busy city returned.

"Helen, you and Robert all right?"

"Yes, Kora," said Helen still holding Kora's cell phone in her shaking hand.

"Please do not make any calls on that phone. Especially not to the penthouse. The police will come and I'll tell them about the other cars in the garage, they need to be checked for bombs. But I want what happened here to be as quiet as possible for as long as possible. We need to get to the airport. Actually I think we should fly the main terminal and take a regular flight."

"The laptop and the luggage?" asked Helen as she handed Kora the cell phone.

"It's fine," said Kora over the loud sirens of the police, fire trucks and ambulance. "It's only stuff, and stuff can be replaced, people can't. I'll talk to the cops, then we'll get going to grand-mother's house in Berlin and find out what is going on.

"Helen, are there any calls from the family yet?" She asked as she straightened her black denim slacks and brushed off her soft light jacket.

"No, Princess," answered Helen shivering in the rain. Turing away form where her car disappeared into the water she saw the Chief of Police come toward where they were standing.

Kora raised her chin and put on her regal smile as rain streamed down her face. She waited for Chief Morgan trying to think how she might explain this.

"Princess Kora, it's good to see you again. I see what looks like your Rolls over there in the creek. Can you tell me what's going on?" The chief eyed Kora, Helen and Robert in their dirty, wet clothing.

Their hair was disheveled with bits of road and weeds mixed in with their normal elegant coiffures. Luckily they didn't have many road burns on their faces, only a few knees and elbow or two of clothing were missing.

"Yes, Chief, as you surmised, that is my Rolls in the water. We noticed there was a bomb under it as we exited the garage and drove to where it would do the least damage," said Kora as she started to walk away from where onlookers were gathering. The Chief followed her.

She didn't want her name in the paper, and wanted to keep everything as quiet as she could at least until after she found and retrieved her grandmother.

Kora simplified what had happened with her grandmother, to Robert, and now the bomb.

"If you could have the fence repaired and any damage done by the car and send the bills to me I would be grateful. Also, if you could send the bomb squad to the garage and check out the other cars that would be wonderful. Again, please send any accounting for their hours to me I'll take care of it," said Kora in a soft voice.

"Are you sure that your all right? Is there anything we can do to help you find who planted this bomb?" asked the Chief solicitously.

"Thank you but no." She hesitated. "Actually there might be. Would it be possible you might have an unmarked car that could take us to International Departures at the airport? Right now?" asked Kora trying to keep a straight face and control of her emotions. But she realized there was a traffic jam and the sooner they got to the airport the better.

"Certainly, Princess, I'll get one of the plain clothes detectives cars to take you right now," said the chief as he waved over a young man and woman.

"Yes, Chief?" asked the young woman as she approached the Chief and the Princess. She was in her twenties wearing jeans, a white tee shirt, and a burgundy hoody.

"Please take the Princess and her friends to VIA International Departures and drop the off," said the Chief to the two officers.

"I'll take care of the other matters too, Princess. Have a safe journey," he said as he looked around at the floating Rolls.

"Thank you, Chief. I think things will be running smoothly from now on," said Kora with a small smile making sure her fangs and talons had been suppressed.

They went directly to Vancouver International Airport in a very quiet car ride and were dropped off by the officers in front of the International Departures area.

"Thank you very much, officers," said Kora as she slid out of the vehicle with Helen and Robert following her murmuring their thanks as well.

"The first thing we need to do is go to the airlines, get emergency passports and book passage on the first flight out of Vancouver going to Berlin. Then cell phones, laptops, and clothing," said Kora to Helen and Robert as they followed her into the terminal. She scowled at her cell phone and even shook it as they went as fast as they could, with people around them all going different directions in the massive airport.

"Stop," ordered Kora as they approached a shorter line up for a European carrier going to Berlin. She checked the departure screen then turned to look at Helen and Robert. "Don't smile," said Kora as she raised her cell phone and took a quick frontal selfie of herself, then pictures of Helen, and Robert.

The approached the fount counter and an airline attendant tried not to look startled as they approached her.

Kora reached into her jacket and pulled out her credit card and put in onto the counter. "We need three first class seats to Berlin on the next available flight."

"May I see your passports?" asked the attendant politely as she glanced at the credit card. She stopped speaking and looked at the Royal credit card marked with the Consortiums crest and her royal's house crest on it.

"Between this card and the pictures on this phone I believe you have everything you'll need to make us three emergency passports and tickets. Correct?" Kora said she put down the cell phone with their pictures showing on the screen.

"Certainly, that would be my privilege," said the attendant bobbing her head and checking her computer screen.

She motioned for her supervisor to come over and whispered in his ear. He smiled at Kora as he gave her back the credit card and phone.

"Please come with me and I'll get you settled in our VIP lounge while we get this taken care for you. Please follow me," he said as he led them away.

Soon they were in the first class lounge taking hot welcoming showers and drying off. They had gone for a quick shop and were now each equipped with a cell phone, computer, clothes and carry-ons. Also in their pockets were brand new passports and first class tickets for Berlin.

They all kept a look out for any other surprises, or anyone else trying to stop them from getting to Berlin.

"Princess, may I help you in contacting the family?" asked Helen as she pulled out her computer.

"No, there are codes that are unique to me that you don't have. I'll take care of it," said Kora as she continued to check her old cell phone.

Kora even tried and used her new cell phone to text her grandmothers castle and her other relatives. There was no response, even when she used her urgent family codes, which should have overridden everything. Reinhold, her grandmother valet should have been in touch with her the minute there was even the slightest suggestion that something was wrong with grandmother. Those were his orders from her, grandmother and the rest of the family. She was the number one contact with all of them.

She was growing agitated and nervous sitting here doing nothing was getting harder and harder as she tried to keep herself under control and not worry.

———

Ten hours later they finally arrived in Berlin after a connecting flight through Frankfurt, it was early evening and Kora's strength was at it's fullest. She could still walk in the open during the day, unlike the old vampire stories she would not burst into flame, but it made her tired, while at night she had her full strength and speed.

Soon they were entering the castle grounds in their limousine but there was something wrong. Kora knew something was wrong but couldn't identify it.

When they got out of the vehicle she knew what it was. There was no one here to greet them and the grounds only had the motion sensors and automatic lights on. Where was everyone?

They tucked their belongings in the hall behind the unlocked front entrance. The foyer was round with a large ornate crystal chandelier hanging from the two-story ceiling above them.

"Interesting," said Kora. "The lights are on but it seems no one's home."

"You both stay here," she instructed Helen and Robert. "I'm going to take a quick look around. If you'd like you can wait in the family parlor, just to your right. I'll meet you there." Kora turned and disappeared around the other corner.

Helen and Robert went into the family parlor and had just gotten seated on the plush rust couches when Kora returned.

"I found the servants, their restrained downstairs in the wine cellar but I untied them. They will be up shortly. We'll have to interview them. There's still no sign of Grandmother," said a grim faced Kora.

There was suddenly a noise from outside and a soft din from the stairs downstairs.

"Princess, I think I..." said Helen turned to Kora and Robert.

"Grandmother," said a stern lipped Kora as she turned to open the entrance door wide and there was her grandmother with Princess May, grandmother's sister.

Princess May was dreadfully pale and her normally light blue eyes were black. She smiled at Kora, her canines long and deadly as she waived a small compact gun at Kora, Helen, and Robert motioning them to go into the great hall.

A quick intake of air was all the surprise that Kora showed as she watched her Aunt May. When had she been turned into a hybrid vampire?

Kora remember saying that not everyone could deal with the idea of living forever and that they would have to be very careful on who was selected in the family to join the inner circle.

"Ah, there you are, my darling, I'm so glad you made it. I was beginning to worry," said Princess May grinning at them.

Kora started to take a step forward and May's cold black eyes locked on Kora's.

"Kora, if you take another step I will kill your grandmother. If I understand it correctly she will live forever unless, her heart stops or her brain get scrambled. And this little gun has special bullets—armor piercing bullets I believe they're called—that will do exactly that," said Aunt May.

In the background of the castle Kora could hear that servants getting on with their normal duties.

"Oh, and don't ask. Why wouldn't I want to be immortal? Of course I do. I've been turned now and so will my children and grandchildren. Sweet Gail will be the first I will reward with immortality. We will have our full birthright and not just what you determine, dear sister," said May as she glared at grandmother with loathing and contempt.

"May, you were always such a drama queen," said grandmother as she frowned at May. She shook her head in disgust as she turned and walked toward massive wood burning fireplace. May followed and stood close to her.

"What I don't understand is Kora what took you so long to get here? I thought you were a very good private detective" It's been at least twelve hours since I was kidnapped?" asked grandmother with a slight smile on her lips.

Kora glanced at her grandmother and saw that there were now four armed guards, two on each side of the entry. They couldn't see grandmother but they could see Kora.

"Excuse me, Princess," Helen whispered loudly. "If there's nothing else could I be excused?"

Kora didn't know weather to scream or laugh hysterically. But everyone turned to look at her.

"What?" intoned Kora, she was stunned.

"Everyone down on the ground," shouted Kora as she dove into grandmother. The tackle carried her and grandmother a good twenty feet from the fireplace where she had been standing next to Aunt May.

When the kill shot came from Aunt May they were both starting to stand up and brush themselves off well out of range.

The guards in their civilian dress with guns drawn came into the hall. They turned in unison and shot down Aunt May. She lay on her back her unseeing eyes gazing at an eternity she hadn't planned for.

"Grandmother, are you ready to go to Switzerland tomorrow? I have to make sure your delivered to the meeting," said Kora as she smoothed down her hair.

"Of course, dear. I'm looking forward to it," said grandmother her dark eyes glowed with pride.

Reinhold, grandmother's butler entered the room. "Madam, the computer server has now been fixed and all messages are now going through. Is there anything I can bring you? Brandy, sherry, whisky?"

"Helen, you may leave. But do come back and join us for a drink on this dark night," said Kora.

Kora looked at her grandmother and they both started to laugh.

THE BEAST OF CADBORO BAY

The Beast of Cadboro Bay

Russ Crossley

C harley Ispaymilt of the Lekwungen squatted on his haunches on the rock-strewn beach idly tossing pebbles he found into the calm waters of Cadboro Bay creating circular patterns in the water. The clear seawater lapped gently against the shoreline.

Charley wondered if his friend would again appear as he had for the past two seasons. The smells of spring grasses and wild flowers filled his senses. Today was the warmest so far this season. The sun and the soft breezes pushed away memories of the harsh cold winds that washed over the island from the south and west each winter.

His heart was heavy this day. The most recent rumor being

circulated among the people was that they would once again be relocated, but this time they would return to their ancestral home in Cadboro Bay. The British named the bay after the first Hudson's Bay Company vessel anchored off then Fort Camosun in 1842. The fort was later renamed Fort Victoria. Or so his teacher at the white man's school told him and his other classmates.

Charley's father didn't believe the rumor because he didn't trust the white men who ruled this place. Charley didn't know if it was true or not. But for a boy of eight seasons he didn't know enough of his elder's ways to decide for himself. All he knew of the people's history was that most of his people had died in the last century.

His grandfather told him there were now five large families and a few smaller ones comprising the entirety of the Lekwungen people.

He glanced up from studying a smooth chalk white rock he'd found on the beach to peer at the wide expanse of ocean running to the horizon. He froze when he spotted the large smooth greenish head and dark eyes sticking just above the surface moving rapidly toward him creating a wake as it cut through the water. His heart beat faster and his mouth became dry. He slowly rose to a standing position letting the pebbles in his hands drop onto the rocky beach with a clatter.

It had to be hiyitl'iik returning to bay as its kind had since the creation of the world. Charley called his friend Robert, which the beast readily agreed to when they first met two seasons before.

Robert stopped just off shore his head now sticking well above the surface of the blue water. "Hello, Charley," the sea creature said in its gravelly voice.

"Hello, Robert, it is good to see you again." When the creature first spoke in the language of the people Charley had been afraid he might have died and not known it. But as their conversation grew Charley realized he wasn't dead or dreaming. This creature of legend was very real and was really speaking to him in his own language.

Robert's head reminded Charley of a horse's, without ears or nostrils, but its eyes were in front of its head, which was flat just like a horse.

Robert bowed his head slightly. "It is nice to see you once again as well."

"What shall we talk about this year?" asked Charley genuinely curious how this sea creature knew so much about the people.

"Perhaps you can start by explaining where the rest of the people are? I thought you might bring more of them to meet me. I only come to this bay once a year."

Charley sighed inwardly. The people were now very small in number. How would this creature react? "The people are busy preparing for another relocation. The white rulers have determined where we live is not good." He shrugged. "I told my father and mother about you but they didn't believe me. My father took the strap to me for lying..."

Robert's features shifted and twitched. Charley didn't know what that meant. "I am sorry to cause you trouble," Robert said after a few uncomfortable seconds of silence between them.

"My father beats me all the time. Sometimes he doesn't have a reason. It's no problem."

Robert's features again shifted this time to his normal placid features. He was obviously relieved. "Your father is very strict." Charley nodded then changed the topic. "This year I would enjoy telling you about the origins of the people and how I and your ancestors became forever linked."

What followed was a long tale beginning with the dangerous journey the people made from the far north to the coast of what was now British Columbia. The people ended their journey settling on the lower half of Vancouver Island and few decades numbered in the many thousands.

Charley felt as if he was being carried away in the words drawn to another time and place. Finally he blinked and realized the sun was high in the sky. His father would be looking for him. The store would be busy with customers and he expected every member of the family to contribute.

"I must leave, Robert," he said interrupting the creature who was about to relate his tale of the arrival of the white people from far away lands across the vast oceans.

Robert eyed him with his black eyes that were reflecting what seemed to Charley like compassion. I must be dreaming. "If you must go...I will see you again next year."

Charley smiled wistfully. "Yes, of course." The sea creature disappeared beneath the water and was gone. Charley was enveloped by a deep sense of regret mingled with loss. He turned away and starting running across the open ground toward the people's community.

What he didn't know at the time is he wouldn't see Robert again until eight seasons had come and gone.

———

Charley stood by the waters edge staring out over the expanse of dark water. The sun was low in the sky and the breeze was churning up the bay creating small white caps. The smell of the salt water washed over him.

"Hello, Charley," said a familiar voice that made him freeze where he stood. Glancing to his left he saw Robert staring at him with those dark eyes. "It has been eight seasons."

Charley nodded and cleared his throat. He swallowed his fear and said, "Hello, Robert, I thought you weren't real. I thought I'd make you up." This beast was speaking the language of the people his late grandmother had taught him. Speaking their language in public was dangerous and some whites considered it illegal. This is what he'd been taught at the residential school he'd lived at for the past eight years up island.

The creature chuckled in an odd way that wasn't exactly human. "I'm very real, Charley." The sea creature paused. "Do you remember what we talked about?"

"Yes," he replied hesitantly. "You told me you are linked to the people. And you told me about the early history of my people." His brow wrinkled. "Did you tell me how we're linked together?"

"No, Charley, you had to leave. Something about your father's store."

Charley smirked. "Yeah. My father."

"Did I say something wrong?"

"No. Not at all. My father is dying. That's why I left school. Someone has to keep the store running and my family elected me."

"I'm so sorry to hear your father is unwell," said Robert his head bobbing in the choppy ocean.

I'm not, thought Charley. His father beat him for years and he let him be taken away to the school where the brothers beat him just about as frequently. He knew of boys who were touched in their private areas, but given how he had grown so large and muscular in the past three years, and was now captain of both the cricket and rugby teams, the brothers at the school left him alone.

Charley decided to change the subject. Talk of his brutal father and the brothers brought back terrible images and had formed a knot of tension in his belly. "Tell me about the connection between us and you."

Robert nodded. "When the people first arrived in this area they began fishing the waters for food. A member of my kind became entangled in their fishing nets. They pulled him ashore right on this beach and realized they had made a mistake. They displayed such regret and kindness to my ancestor that he pledged my kind would defend the people against any aggressor."

Charley's brow wrinkled and he arched at eyebrow at the water serpent. The beginnings of a knot of anger formed in his belly. "Then why did your kind let the white people invade our land?"

Robert was silent for several seconds. Finally he said, "They were not aggressive toward the people. They appeared to come in peace. They brought gifts and technology. We thought your gentle people would befriend these strangers from across the oceans. They like the people are Homo sapiens—you are all the same species."

"You seem to know a lot about these white men." Charley looked away toward the horizon where the sun seemed to be settling into the ocean the sky now streaked with gold and orange hues. "They brought death and slavery to the people. They brought some good things, but much more terrible suffering than anything else. They passed laws making our traditional ways unlawful and our gods they called heathen. Our spoken language is also illegal." His eyes narrowed. "Which means this conversation is breaking the white man's laws."

The beasts coal black eyes reflected its surprise. "I had no idea how bad it has become for the people. I wish we could do more."

"You can't...or won't?"

Robert's eyes drooped and Charley felt a twinge of regret for speaking so bluntly. Robert had been very open and kind to him since they first met all those years ago. Charley had been unable to confirm the relationship between the people and the hiyitl'iik though his late grandmother did say the people were attuned to the earth and the spirits of all living things around them.

"I'm sorry, Robert. None of this is your fault." Charley stuffed his hands in the pockets of his blue jeans. "Maybe we should fight the whites..." His voice trailed off as he thought about the white man's weapons. The people had none of these weapons.

He had seen the news reel footage of the Great War and saw the awful destruction they were capable of when fighting an enemy. If the white rulers began to see the people as an enemy... no, violence was not the answer.

"My kind has tried to fight the whites in the past. We failed. Many died," said Robert his voice low and tinged with sorrow.

Charley's was nearly overcome by the grief emanating from this gentle creature. His people, including him, were very much in tune with other living things. "What do you suggest we do?"

Robert didn't say anything for several seconds. Charley had the impression he was gathering his thoughts and considering the options. Finally he spoke. "You will go to school and learn how to become a ruler among the people. Then you will engage with the whites and use their own ways to build mutual respect for both sides."

Charley was shocked by the response. "I can't. I have to work at my father's store. I must serve my family."

"Yes. For now," agreed Robert. "But you have a younger brother I believe."

Charley nodded. "Yes, my brother, Stephen. He is five seasons younger."

"Yes, then he will take over the business once you leave to further your education."

Charley scoffed. "This is nonsense. The whites will never allow me to participate in higher education."

"We shall see, my dear Charley. We shall see."

———

After another ten seasons had passed before Charley returned to Cadboro Bay. This time he wasn't alone. Due to the steady rain he'd brought an umbrella. The steady breeze threatened to damage the umbrella at any moment.

As had happened before Robert—now dubbed The Beast of Cadboro Bay by local white fishermen and the newspapers—met them as they approached the waters edge. The people maintained the myths about the creature to the whites when asked, but maintained their friendship with Robert and the others of his kind. The truth was the whites would never have believed the people if they were told the truth. They would have dismissed the legends as primitive Indian superstition.

"Good to see you again, Robert," said Charley his wife squeezing his left arm tightly upon seeing the massive snake like shape of the hiyitl'iik 's gray-green coils cresting the waves of the bay. Due to the rain the bay was deserted except for Charley, his new bride, and of course, Robert.

"Hello, Charley," replied the sea serpent. Charley's wife slipped behind him apparently uneasy upon seeing the mythical creature in the flesh. She peered past him.

"It's okay, Maggie, he is real as I told you. His name is Robert." Charley turned to grasp her hand in his and gently pulling her forward to stand beside him. He enveloped her trembling shoulder in his long arm and wrapped his fingers around where her slender arm met her shoulder. He gazed into her wide eyes, a gentle smile on his lips. "There is nothing to fear. He is a friend to the people."

He turned back to face Robert the ancient creature's massive body bobbing in the wind churned surf. "Robert, this is my new wife, Margaret. She is of the Shishalh people."

Maggie waved at Robert and smiled weakly. Her dark brown eyes and coal black hair were common features of her people, as was her skin the color of coffee with a dollop of cream. Charley was at least five inches taller than her.

Robert bowed his head slightly in greeting. "So nice to meet you, Margaret."

"You may call me Maggie," she suddenly blurted out her voice quivering with fear. "He calls me Maggie...my family, and my friends, call me Maggie." Robert appeared pleased his eyes sparkling in the gloom.

"I wanted to thank you in person," said Charley breaking the moment.

"Oh?" said Robert. "For what?" His horse like head bobbed in the light chop in the bay. The weather had turned for the worse, darker clouds filled the horizon accompanied by ever-stronger winds.

"A white man named Winston Peters sponsored my entrance into the University. I recently graduated with a law degree." Charley could not keep the deep pride he felt from his voice. The people were taught to be humble and refrain from boasting, but his accomplishment would allow him to change his people's future for the better. And this deserved some recognition.

"Wonderful!" said Robert. "But what has this to do with me?"

"When I asked why he sponsored me Mr. Peters told me a friend urged him to help me in any way he could." Before Robert could say anything Charley added, "He refused to tell me the name of the friend." He shrugged. "I assumed it was you...somehow..."

A sudden gust of wind blew Charley's umbrella inside out. Maggie yelped and covered her head with her arms. "Com'on, Charley, we have to leave." She turned away and began to walk briskly toward the stand of trees in the park that ran the length of the beach behind them.

"Will you tell me please?" Charley shouted over the now howling wind and the roar of rainfall striking the rocks and sand around him.

"Next time, Charley." Robert disappeared beneath the waves

just as flash of lightning shot across the gray rain streaked sky followed by a rolling thunder.

———

After seventeen seasons passed until Charley again appeared at the beach on Cadboro Bay. A few billowy white clouds dotted the otherwise blue early morning sky. The ocean was calm, the surface rippled by a slight breeze coming from the southwest. In the distance were a sailboat and a freighter moved slowly into the straight. The smells of the sea filled his senses as it had all those years ago when he first met his friend at this place.

The population of Victoria had dramatically grown in the years after the Second World War. Now the forested lands bordering the bay had been designated as part of the Cadboro-Gyro Park by the city and the district of Saanich. This meant the stand of tall pine trees that dotted the green parklands would obscure people's view of the bay. It was early on a Tuesday morning so Charley hoped he and Robert could meet with some guarantee of privacy.

While the people would know what Robert was the whites would fear him and might harm him since they thought of him a mindless beast.

"Hello, Charley," said the familiar voice.

The creature's head appeared just off shore to his right. Charley couldn't help but grin. His heart beat rapidly. He was secretly thrilled to see his old friend. "Robert! I'm so happy to see you..." His voice trailed off replaced by a sense of dread when he realized Robert's green and gray flesh looked wizen and his black eyes reflected his weakened condition. He was sick. Maybe even dying.

"Robert?"

The creature moved slightly his coils rising and falling in the water creating a small wake. "My time is near," he said simply his voice sounding weaker than he recalled. "This will be the last time we will meet."

A single tear rolled down Charley's cheek and a sense of grief swept over him. Not wanting to add to his friend's misery he sucked in a breath to steady himself and changed subjects. "Maggie is well. She sends her regards but today is my oldest sons graduation day and she wanted to stay behind to make the breakfast for our three children and prepare the house for the celebration party."

"That sounds wonderful," said Robert. "I too have children. Two."

Charley could not hide his surprise. "Really? We never talked about it." He realized then he had been selfish in the past only caring about his and the people's needs. "I'm sorry..." His voice trailed off.

"There is nothing to be sorry for, Charley. You and I are friends and it is my duty to assist the people for the great kindness and respect they have shown to my kind over the millennia." Robert paused. "I know you've away wondered who the friend was who told Winston Peters to sponsor your admittance to the University."

Charley could barely contain his excitement. This question had eluded him for decades. He really wanted to know.

"Your father was once a fisherman was he not?"

Charley nodded, but wondered what his father had to do with this. His late father died many years ago and had been a terrible man who beat him and belittled him terribly all his life.

"Your father rescued a white man named Winston Peters from drowning during a storm when they were both young men. Winston was wealthy and connected to the white rulers. It was he who sponsored your father so he could buy the store."

"A member of my kind called Anthony befriended your father

when he was a fisherman and they met in this very bay as we do for many years. Before he passed away, at the suggestion of Anthony, your father urged Winston to help his son in anyway possible. It was Winston who convinced the University to accept you given your above average academic success."

My father? Charley could not believe his ears. How could it be? "So your kind and my father conspired to get me into university? To make my life more like the white rulers?"

"No. You earned your degree on your own merit, with hard work and dedication, not to become like the white rulers but to make changes to benefit your people. To make them free of the white rulers."

"I must think about this, Robert. This changes everything."

"Yes, I know which is why I tell you now at the end of my time."

A wave of guilt swept over Charley. Here he was again thinking of himself first instead of his friend. "I'm so sorry, Robert. Is there anything I can do for you?"

"Just remember me," said Robert before he slipped beneath the waves and was gone.

———

Thirty-three seasons later Charley gazed forlornly from his seat on the park bench at the foam topped white caps streaming toward the beach along Cadboro Bay. The wind gusted and the air smelled like rain and charged ozone. A storm was on the way.

He pulled up the collar of his thick waterproof coat around his neck and coughed. A seagull swept by overhead is cry mournful cry matching his mood. it appeared to be flying inland away from the incoming weather. The seas birds weren't fools.

He tugged the brim of his driving cap down as light rain began to fall from a steel gray sky. The cup of coffee he held in his left hand had created a film in his mouth. He licked his lips as a sense of sadness fell over him. No sign again this year of his friend.

Robert was indeed dead. And had been for many years. Charley didn't want to accept the loss. Legends never died. Myths never died.

He tossed the disposable coffee cup in the trash bin next to the bench rose to his feet and stuffed his hands in the pockets of his blue jeans. It was time to give up. To go home. His eyes were cast down at the blacktopped walkway running along the beach as he started walking.

"Are you, Charley?" said a deep voice behind him.

Charley froze where he stood then after sucking in a deep breath turned around and saw what at first appeared to be Robert bobbing in the water. His brow wrinkled as his brown eyes scanned the serpent like creature looking back at him with its coal black eyes. The pattern of the colors on its coils visible above the waves didn't look right. They were different somehow.

Could it be? "Yes, I'm Charley." He paused and his heart rate increased as excitement grew from the pit of his belly. "Are you a child of Robert?"

"Yes, I am. You may call me Amy."

"Why are you here?" asked Robert his trembling hands now free of his pants pockets.

"Before he passed my father asked me to continue this tradition and to let you know your children will be greater than you can ever imagine."

While Charley had been a good lawyer, but continuing systemic prejudices by the white rulers made his time difficult, he was retired now. His two sons were in law school and would soon graduate. His son's accomplishments were all that was left of his pride of being a lawyer fighting for the people. He had too often thought of himself as a failure.

"How do you know?" he asked his desperation evident in his voice.

"We will help you as we always have. My father also wanted you to know you were never a failure. You were the defender of the people and your descendants will be encouraged by your success."

Charley considered the creature's words and a sense of calm came over him. The Beast of Cadboro Bay was a friend of the people and always would be.

WAR EAGLE

Rita Schulz

Ruby Eagle, known to her close friends as Ruby Flare, was an international hero, a diminutive but fierce hummingbird. She stretched out her hand, just this once, to gently touch the orange-and-yellow sleek, tight-fitting uniform she used to wear.

She loved the way the red sparkly accent fabric at the throat shimmered in the light. It looked full of life. Ready to go. She ran her hand over the smooth, hard metal surface of her rocket pack with its green leather harness and wondered if she would ever use it to fly again.

She eyed the smaller uniform next to hers. It was green and blue, with the same deep red throat. Her greatest wish was that her daughter Anna would take her place as a Hummingbird, an elite division of the Atlantean War Eagles, but Anna was completely against the idea. She didn't want to even hear the old stories and legends of the great Atlanteans and their history.

Ruby closed the shatterproof, sparkling clean glass case, turned, and slowly limped away, trying not to lean on her smooth red arbutus cane as she stepped back.

It had been a long time since she had been in her secret space. Her large, hidden workroom contained her uniforms, weapons, and computers. It was an area about twelve feet by eighteen feet, a good-sized room specifically designed to have it's own private entrance besides the one in her closet—two of them in fact, one from a balcony and the other from her private elevator. Outside her workroom in the penthouse, there wasn't a trace of the entry. In fact, there was no indication a hidden room existed.

She stepped into her closet and pushed the wooden panel that closed the doorway to her hidden workroom.

The closet, with all its clothes, different textures, and colors, shifted and drifted around her as she walked through it into her bedroom. The smell of roses and lavender softly enveloped her as she walked.

The morning news echoed from the radio next to her bed. The world was in turmoil. It needed true leadership and heroes more than ever. She held back the tears filling her eyes and threatening to spill down her cheeks. She held back the grief as she chose the clothes she would wear today. An aqua long sleeved shirt with comfortable black leggings seemed to fit her mood.

The aqua looked wonderful with her dark blonde hair and green eyes, and the leggings suited her petite, slender figure.

She went to her nightstand and checked her cell phone. Good. No calls. It had been quiet over the last week. Just the way she liked it. No news was good news.

She looked in her full-length mirror and debated whether to tie back her shoulder-length hair as the apartment doorbell rang, interrupting her thoughts. Then she heard a key turn in the lock. Ruby knew it must be her daughter Anna. Anna always rang first to let her knew someone was there so she wouldn't be startled, then used her key to enter the apartment.

She looked at the time. What had happened? Somehow she had lost an hour. That can't be correct. There was no way she had been staring at the uniform, dreaming her life away for an hour. It was a life she had never wanted.

"Mom, Mom! Are you here?" called her daughter as she entered the spacious apartment. The large picture windows facing the sun-washed False Creek provided breathtaking views and plenty of light, bathing the room in a glow. There was every kind of vessel in the harbor, from small people ferries to magnificent yachts moving as if in a chaotic ballet.

"I'm in the bedroom, Anna," Ruby called as she put her super power of speed to the test and was dressed in less than three seconds. She smiled when she walked out of the bedroom, smoothing her hair as she hurried to the hallway.

"Are you okay, Mom? You look kind of flushed. And you didn't answer your cell when I called earlier," asked Anna as she tipped her head to one side causing her shoulder-length dark blonde hair to fall over one shoulder. She studied her mother carefully, her brow wrinkled.

"Oh, I'm fine. Everything is good. Time just got away from me. Where do you want to go for lunch?" Ruby said as she opened the hall coat closet and pulled out a light blue rain jacket, which she slipped on, then pulled out her gray leather cross-body purse and slipped it over her head, draping it comfortably across her body. She glanced at her cane and her lips formed a thin line. She hated the stupid thing but knew if she didn't take it, Anna would comment on it. Or worse, pick it up and hand it to her.

Why did Anna insist on giving her such a hard time? She was doing everything that the stupid physiotherapist told her to do, but the strength to her right leg still wasn't coming back and her balance was off, too. After a year and a half, she felt like she would never be able to walk properly again, never mind fly, land and fight smoothly with her rocket pack. She was a superhero who was grounded and her power of super speed was only good for getting dressed in a hurry. What a stupid waste.

"Anna, I was thinking I would stay home from the council meeting in Berlin this year. I've been to every meeting over the last twenty-eight years. That's six times in a row, not counting all the special meetings. We have other approved members who can go in my place." She checked her jacket pockets for her keys. They weren't there.

She shook her body bag and heard the jangling sound and smiled. She really should get one of the clickers that were so popular with her friends, but she thought those things were stupid. It was as if her friends were getting old and couldn't remember anything. At forty-seven years of age, she certainly wasn't old and neither were her friends. They were just lazy and couldn't be bothered to try remembering. They didn't exercise their minds at all.

Anna's eyebrows furrowed as she looked at her mother with concern all over her narrow features.

"Look, Mom, we don't have to go out for lunch if you don't want to. You need time to figure this all out."

"What are you talking about, Anna?"

Anna paused before she answered her mother. Her expression shifted between shocked and confused.

"Mom, our representation for the Atlanteans in the leading five hundred families is hanging on by a thread," said Anna as she went into the kitchen and poured herself a glass of cool tea from a jug in the fridge.

"Anna, I don't know what you're talking about. We are well represented this year, only missing a few people. The Grays are in Africa on a working holiday."

"What? You do know that four of our members have recently died and three are on holidays. Yes, the Grays are serving in Africa with the Doctors Without Borders; that only leaves one more qualified representative. If something happens to them, well.... You have to go," said Anna, her tone firm.

"I haven't heard anything about members dying," said Ruby. "They would have called me. I'm the family's first contact person. Everything like that would go through me."

"Mom, I've been calling you. A couple of times this morning, too, and you haven't been answering. The messages go right to voice mail, and the last time I tried to leave you a message, your answering service said your mailbox was full. What's going on?" said Anna as she crossed her arms over her chest. She finished her tea and set the glass in the sink.

Ruby nodded at her daughter, watching her eyes carefully. Was Anna trying to play a trick on her? She looked at her cell phone, tapped her code into it, and slowly put the phone to her ear. There were twenty-two missed calls and ten of them were marked urgent. Something was very wrong with her phone.

"Oh dear. I see what you mean. Just give me a minute to check my messages." Ruby ambled into the large second bedroom that doubled as a guest bedroom and her office.

The walls were painted light gray with a soft blue-gray feature wall. The room was comfortable and relaxing. Two of the walls were lined in warm oak bookshelves full of books. Another wall had an oak roll-top desk and two chairs on the sides of the desk, one a stationary chair and the other a rolling leather office chair.

She pulled up the top of the roll-top, laid her phone on the desktop, then pulled the office chair in place and picked up a pen and pad of paper lying on the desktop.

Ruby quickly took notes as she went through the messages. Some she deleted and others she forwarded to her computer and special files.

Anna stood silently in the doorway, watching. Finally she said, "Mom, is there something I can do to help?"

Ruby glanced up and shook her head until she once more focused on her messages and notes.

Ruby's secret desire was that Anna would take up her position in the War Eagle Council and on the council of the Five Hundred Families. Anna's position was one of inheritance through Ruby, and before that, her grandmother. But until now Anna had refused anything to do with her inheritance, including her gifts as an Atlantean.

Anna had inherited the natural quick agility, speed, and balance that was far superior to average humans and something she always hid when among normal humans. Even Ruby didn't know the true extent of Anna's gifts since they differed greatly from person to person.

Ruby held her desire for her daughter close to her heart and very seldom mentioned it around her. Ruby knew the more she pushed, the more Anna would do the opposite.

Ruby also knew for Anna to commit to the council and take her place as royalty in the War Eagle clan, and more importantly the Meeting of the Five Hundred, Anna would need to do so without any coaxing from her mother.

These life-changing decisions were something Ruby's mother had left for her to decide as well. Her mother told that if she took on the position, her life would change immediately and forever. There was no going back, no change of mind later, no abdicating. It was big stuff.

Ruby realized that she did not have the time she needed to find out all the details of what had been happening with the family. She would have to prioritize to take care of the largest concerns.

She checked the dates on her messages and realized she had been out of touch for twenty-four hours. How had that happened?

She remembered going out for dinner with her sister Marana the night before—they had never been close, but got along fine. They had gone for Japanese food, one of her favorites, at a local place she had eaten at regularly for years.

"Mom, are you okay?" asked Anna.

"Yes, I'm fine." Ruby changed the subject. "I was just thinking about what happened last night."

"Well, what happened?"

"Nothing much. Marana came over and we went out for dinner at Sushi's on Main. I had a bento box and brought half of it home. The only thing different from my usual dinner was that we had some saké."

"You had a drink? That's fine, not something you do all the time, but every once in a while," said Anna. She disappeared back into the kitchen and Ruby heard the sounds associated with her daughter making tea.

"Yes, I know," Ruby called after her, "but the strange thing was that Marana ordered it and when it came, she poured it for me but she didn't have any herself. She filled my little porcelain cup a few times, but not hers."

Anna walked back into the office. She shrugged. "Maybe she decided she didn't feel like it. You know she's flighty. I'm surprised you had dinner with her actually. A family dinner I understand, but not a private dinner. How is Shannon, my dear cousin?" Anna went back into the kitchen to get fresh tea bags out of the cupboard. Ruby followed her.

"I know you've never gotten along with Shannon."

"I got along with her just fine until I realized Shannon couldn't be trusted and neither could Aunt Marana. They really are an interesting line of the family. Our family is considered royalty and don't care or really want the family and international obligation, and they really, really want it." Anna poured hot water into the teapot to warm it.

"Yes, you're right. We have the obligation and they don't, so that's why the job looks so glamorous to them and they covet it. It must seem like no work and only fun for us." Ruby sat down at the round blond maple kitchen table.

Ruby ran her fingertips over the smooth, light-colored, warm wood. She loved the feel of it. It was as if it were alive and was one of the few pieces she still had from Atlantis.

Anna brought the tea and mugs to the table. They both took their tea black so it was very simple.

"Thank you, Anna," Ruby said as Anna poured the tea. Ruby put her hands around the warm mug to comfort herself.

"Mom," Anna began, her eyes serious. "There's something we need to discuss." After a short pause she continued. "It's something I didn't think I would ever talk to you about." Anna picked up her teacup and took a sip.

Ruby took a small sip of her tea as she calmed and centered herself. She was determined she would not show any emotion, good or bad, at what Anna was about to tell her. All she could do was hope. She waited.

"I spoke with Shannon—actually, she spoke with me—she wants to take your place on the council. Before you freak, let me finish," said Anna, looking into her mother's eyes pleadingly.

Ruby looked at the tabletop as she lifted her hands up and steepled them. She took in slow, deep breaths. Rage started to build in her belly. How dare Shannon contact Anna and tell her daughter she wanted Ruby's position on the council. The girl was a greedy airhead and it always seemed all she wanted to do was party.

Ruby slowly locked eyes with her daughter.

"What are you saying, Anna?" Her tone sounded menacing even to her.

Anna appeared unfazed. "I think I need to go with you to the council meeting this year and find out about who I am, as an Atlantean, and what your position entails. I need to find out exactly what I'm thinking of turning down before my dear cousin Shannon tries to take it. When do we leave?" asked Anna, smiling faintly at her mother.

Ruby recognized a faint glimmer of fear in Anna's eyes and she nodded to reassure her daughter.

———

A few weeks later, Ruby packed her things and asked Anna to back up her computer and email and pack those to take with them too. They would stop off at Anna's modest apartment to pick up her things and then they would be off.

"Mom, can I drive the car? Please? You've been saying maybe for a very long time and you're with me right now," pleaded Anna as they took Ruby's apartment elevator to the parking garage where her vintage red mustang convertible was parked. With a grin, Anna grabbed the car keys from her mother's hand and dropped the keys into her own light green jacket.

They'd take it to the airport.

Ruby shook her head as she watched the young girl who along the way had changed from her daughter into a talented young woman.

Anna was now a successful fiction writer, just like her mother. It had been a long time since Ruby had realized Anna was an adult—since her twenty-fifth birthday, and that had been three years ago.

Ruby took a deep breath and nodded. Unable to contain her excitement, Anna whooped with joy and gave her mother a quick hug as she swung the driver's door open after putting their suitcases in the trunk.

They both slipped into the car's tan leather seats, gently hugged by the luxurious interior.

"Now remember, this is a very special car," cautioned Ruby. A long time ago she'd had the car modified so it was one of the fastest cars on the road—and one of the only things she had left from her husband, who had died ten years ago in an accident when his rocket pack stalled during high aerial practice.

"I know, Mom," said Anna, then gave the candy apple red, black-roofed convertible a little more gas than was needed, causing the powerful car to lurch slightly. She laughed as she braked to a stop, shifted into reverse, then back into drive and drove out of the garage onto the street.

It was a beautiful, warm, sunny day in Vancouver. The sky was blue with a few high white clouds—a perfect summer day.

They arrived at the airport in less than half an hour and Anna smiled warmly at the long-term parking attendant. Once they were parked, they took out their suitcases and flagged down the shuttle to take them to the international terminal for their flight to Berlin.

Ruby gazed at Anna. Her eyes were sparkling and her cheeks glowed. Her daughter was obviously excited. She had been to Berlin before as a visitor, but Ruby knew this was going to be a different kind of trip for her. Something special.

They would be in Berlin for two weeks and Anna would have to listen and learn a lot of new things she had purposefully not wanted to learn before.

Nine hours later they arrived in Berlin after a very comfortable trip. Anna loved being in business class—her first time—Ruby had splurged on them both.

Ruby wondered if her sisters, nieces and nephews, and cousins would show up at the meeting or just use this as a trip to go shopping or traveling, which was their usual excuse for their summer holiday.

The excitement and apprehension grew like a peach pit in Ruby's belly. Anna was facing a massive learning curve and a decision that would mean her life would change forever. Would both their lives change? Of course her life would change was she ready to do that? Not be the leader? What would happen if and when Ruby's standing in the family changed and a new leader was chosen? How would she feel? What would she do especially if she couldn't be a Hummingbird warrior?

Ruby sat next to Anna at the baggage carousel, waiting for their luggage to come down. She struggled to remain calm, but her heart was beating fast. She hoped she had packed everything they would need, but only time would tell.

Ruby went over and over the information she would have to cover with Anna in her mind. Should she deal with the history of their family first or their abilities? Anna never had liked history growing up. It was one of her worst subjects at school. Ruby kept reminding herself Anna was an adult. Maybe she should just let Anna ask questions on topics, answer them, and make sure that everything was covered.

"Mom, look who's here." Anna said brightly. "It's Shannon and Aunt Marana; why do you think they're here?"

Ruby looked around the busy arrivals area trying to locate their chauffeur.

"Anna! Anna, how are you?" said Shannon as she smiled at Anna and moved in for an air kiss. She stepped back and arched a disapproving eyebrow at Ruby. "Hello, Aunt Ruby, I see you've both come to Berlin. What are you doing here?" Shannon asked Ruby with a strange glint in her eyes.

Anan spoke first, her lips forming a tight line. "We're here for the meeting, at least Mom is. What are you doing here? Shopping?" She stole a glance at her mother, who gave a slight shake of her head.

"How are you, Shannon?" asked Ruby, her attention on their

surroundings, trying to spot their chauffer among the crowd of passengers.

"I guess you haven't heard," said Shannon with a smirk on her lips. "You were too busy, I assume? There's an open spot for another representative on the council since the Amazons are no longer a voting group."

The Atlanteans and the Amazons usually voted together as the Peace Delegation and sought to bring better solutions to the table of the Five Hundred.

Ruby's heart hammered hard. If this was true, there would be trouble—and she hadn't heard back from one of their own representatives. She would have to make sure that they had their own quorum at the next meeting.

Ruby caught Anna's attention with a nod. "Stay here with our luggage and keep your eyes open for the driver," Ruby said. She spoke low so only Anna would hear over the crowd noise, then shifted her attention to her niece.

"Yes, Shannon. Thank you for letting us know the news. Have a nice holiday and say hello to your mother. Are you staying at the Royal Gardens?"

Shannon nodded, offering Ruby an insincere smile.

Before she left them, Ruby noticed the pulse on Shannon's throat and realized she was extremely excited and struggling to hide her feelings.

"Yes, we'll be there. See you soon," said Shannon with a pout on her lips as she glared at them before she turned and walked away toward her mother.

"You're doing very well," Ruby assured her daughter. "We'll talk more when we get into our hotel rooms." The crowds began to dissipate and Ruby grinned when she saw their chauffer holding a placard with their names on it not far from the exit doors.

The chauffer came over with two baggage carts and started to load their luggage. Ruby saw the man's grim expression as he handled two of their suitcases that she knew were heavy. After all, she had packed them.

Once at the hotel, Ruby and Anna entered their reserved two-bedroom suite. Ruby watched Anna's joyful expression out of the corner of one eye as Anna looked around the double king-size rooms they would be sharing.

It was a large space done in cream and taupe with touches of gold and red; there was a soft scent of roses and lavender in the air. It was a very sumptuous room with two long couches set across from each other, a coffee table in a high gloss mahogany that matched the end tables, and a large dining room table with seating for eight. There was a spectacular crystal chandelier hanging over the table that caught the light, spraying it over the walls and ceiling like glitter.

Anna looked at her mother and grinned as the bellhop opened the two oak doors with etched glass that led to the bedrooms. She stood in awe, gazing upon what would be her room for the duration.

"If you could put those cases into my room it would be very helpful," Anna said to the bellhop as she took hold of the cart she wanted and started to push it into the room on the right side of the suite.

"Thank you, Anna," Ruby said. "I'm sure that...Bernard, yes?" The bellhop nodded. "Can do that for us. Now he knows where we'd like our individual cases."

In a few moments their luggage was stored in the correct rooms and Anna was picking at the fruit basket on the dining room table.

"I see you're hungry," said Ruby gently as she handed the bellhop a generous tip before he closed the main door after himself and left them alone.

Ruby pulled out her cell phone and her laptop and set herself up at the large wooden desk next to the ornate fireplace. Soon she had everything up and running, with her yellow legal pad ready with sticky pads, pens, and pencils.

"First, I need to check on the other representatives for us and make sure they are here or on their way. Then I'll get hold of the Amazon contingent and find out what happened with them and figure our how to rectify it. We need both of our groups to act and vote as the Peace Hummingbirds," said Ruby.

Anna looked at her mother and smiled, her eyes filling with pride as she saw her mother in her take-charge mode.

"I'm sorry about this, Anna. I guess we'll be discussing things and you'll have to learn very quickly. We work on Roberts Rules. Here's my copy." Ruby held up a small, dingy-gray, dog-eared booklet and tossed Anna a bright white one, "and here is a copy for you. You will need to memorize sections of it."

The house phone started to ring at the same time Ruby's cell phone started vibrating. Anna picked up the house phone and started talking on it. Ruby picked up her cell as she slid Anna a legal pad on the dining room table and a couple of pens. Notes, she mouthed.

Anna was glowing, her eyes were bright, and she was taking notes as if she had been doing this her entire life. Ruby was proud of her and very, very glad she had come on this trip. Ruby had a feeling this was going to be the hardest conference she had ever attended.

"Mom, I just got a message from the Gray's," said Anna as she quickly wrote down a note on her legal pad.

"Good, I called them before we left home to ask them to come to Berlin in case we need another alternate."

"Yes, but the message is that they can't make it. There's been an Ebola outbreak in Africa and they can't get their exit visas approved," Anna turned to face her mother.

"But, Mom, that's not the important thing. They tried to get hold of you today and couldn't get through to your phone. They got us on the hotel phone. I don't understand why you're not...just a minute." Anna picked up her cell and dialed Ruby's number. She watched her mother and the cell phone in her mother's right hand intently.

Nothing happened.

"I'm not getting anything, not even a message prompt. Something has happened to your phone. And I think—"

"It started when I went out for dinner with Marana," Ruby interrupted, pursing her lips.

Anna tapped the end button. "Yes, dear Aunt Marana and Shannon are in it together," she growled. "I think they're making a bid for your seat...our seat. We have to stop them. There seems a lot more to these events."

There was a knock on the door, startling them both. Anna got up from the table and went to answer it.

She opened the door to discover a tall man dressed all in black, with a knee-length cape over his black pants and dress shirt. "Is Ruby Eagle, the leader of the house of Atlantis, here? I have a message for her."

Ruby got up, stood tall, and gracefully walked to the door. "I am Ruby Eagle from the house of Atlantis. How can I help you?"

He pulled out a black, heavy, long glove and slapped Ruby's left cheek with it, startling her. "I am here to present you with a request to meet this afternoon in the meadow behind the hotel for a duel with Shannon Brown for the position of representative of the Atlantis War Eagles. Do you accept the challenge?"

Ruby looked confused, dazed. What was happening? Her family had held this seat for the last five generations. They'd never dueled over it.

Anna strode past her mother to approach the messenger.

Once there, she snatched the glove from his hand and slapped him hard across his left cheek, leaving a red mark.

"You may tell Shannon Brown that Anna Eagle accepts the challenge and will be stepping in as Ruby Eagle's champion," Anna said in an assertive manner. She shifted her gaze to Ruby. "Correct, Mother?"

"Anna....I can't let you. It's too dangerous," stammered Ruby as thoughts and memories of her late husband Galvin's death and her own near fatal accident flashed through her mind.

"Mom, trust me. I know what I'm doing."

Ruby nodded, her eyes still not focusing due to the unexpected blow across her face, but she knew she needed to trust her daughter.

"Yes, Anna Eagle is my champion," said Ruby with a resigned tone in her voice.

The messenger nodded, and with a swirl of his black cloak, he was gone to deliver their reply.

"Anna, what are you doing? You can't—"

"Mom, I understand you want to protect me and keep me safe," interjected Anna with a calm but stern voice.

"Don't you talk to me in that tone of voice."

"Mom, come with me." Anna led Ruby toward her bedroom. "I don't want to fight with you, but there are things you need to know." Anna opened her bedroom door and walked to her suitcases. She hadn't had time to put her things away. Ruby walked stiffly from the doorway.

Anna tossed one of her cases on the bed, opened it, and pulled out her hummingbird costume, which she laid on the bed. Then she opened another heavy case and pulled out her rocket pack and put it next to her costume.

"Mom, you don't know this, but I know all about the costumes and the rocket packs."

Ruby stood there, her eyes wide as she nervously licked her lips.

"No, you don't...it can't be..." A knot of tension tightened her stomach. "How did you get that out of my secret workroom?"

"Mom, I've known about your workroom for years—since I was in university. Right after you gave me a house key, I'd wait until you were out and I'd come over to your place and check it out thoroughly."

"But....you can't know. I've been waiting to explain everything to you." Ruby looked at Anna through watery eyes.

"How did you know how to accept a challenge and declare a champion? Where did that idea come from?"

A whisper of a grin passed over Anna's narrow features. "I know you wanted to teach me, and I want you to, but I first went to Grandma and asked her. That's why I spent so much time with her in the last years of her life; that, and I really loved her."

Ruby looked at Anna as if she was seeing her daughter for the first time.

There was a sharp knock on the door. They stared at it, neither of them moving.

Ruby watched Anna disappear in a blur of super speed to the door, pause, then open it. "Anna Eagle, you have been summoned. What say you?"

"I answer and come with you," said Anna as she went into her bedroom and, in a flash, came out dressed in her costume and rocket pack. "Let's go," she said.

"Ruby Eagle?" said the man in the cape. "You have been summoned." He handed Ruby a manila envelope. "This summons is for you and explains why you have been stripped of your seat."

The messenger turned back to Anna, nodded, and they both went down the hall.

Ruby scanned the documents from the envelope as the man left. It said that she was in violation of her position of leader of the remaining Atlanteans. It cited that she was out of contact with her people and had abandoned her position as their leader.

Ruby was so upset that she was shaking. How dare they? She knew that dear Marana and Shannon had something to do with this. Now "all" she had to do was save Anna, an untrained War Eagle, from battling her cousin, and restore her representative seat with the War Eagles in time for the conference of the Five Hundred.

With Anna gone, Ruby decided she, too, needed to adopt her superhero persona. Her costume and rocket pack were also in her luggage.

Ruby was soon changed and headed to the meadow behind the hotel. She decided to fly; it had been a long time since she had used her rocket pack and it would be marvelous to be flying again.

She discovered there were at least fifty people waiting at the meadow when she arrived overhead but there was no sign of Anna or Shannon. She wondered how they had all found out about the duel. Normally a duel was a quiet, dignified affair and only had the challenger and the responder, with their seconds, in attendance. But this was like a media show. She even noticed cameras, and people also were using their cell phones to record the event. This was going to go viral on the Internet.

Ruby realized that she had forgotten to ask Anna who had trained her in aerial combat. She had mentioned that her grandmother had told her the history, but who had actually made sure she knew how to work the rocket pack?

As Ruby landed a short distance from the field, she heard a loud shout from the people gathered there. She looked over and saw Anna striding toward the meeting area. She had to hurry—Anna didn't have a second. Then she saw Marana come and stand beside Anna.

Ruby's heart hammered. She had trusted Marana at dinner

and with the saké. It seemed that Anna had trusted her aunt as well. What fools they both were.

Ruby watched Anna turn on her rocket pack and it sent her up at a tilted angle to the meadow. When she came down, it was at a steep, sideways angle. She could see the jets on the rocket pack sputter and almost misfire. What was she doing? Then Ruby watched Marana and Shannon start to laugh and realized she and Anna had been completely set up. Anna could die. This wasn't a game. People had died during duels in the past, which is why they were rare these days.

She had to get to her only child. She had to take over for her champion. Ruby was still the Atlantean leader. She had never read anything that said she couldn't take over for her champion at a duel.

She watched as Shannon gracefully rose in the azure sky. Her costume was crimson red and purple, something Ruby had never seen before. Shannon did a few passes around Anna and smiled at Anna's awkward, jerky movements with the rocket pack.

As if a lightbulb had been suddenly turned on, the information fell into place for Ruby. Shannon and Marana were in this together and had sabotaged her communications network. It looked like they had done the same to Anna's training and rocket pack. How could they? They were supposed to be family.

Then she knew her sister's actions were all in the name of jealousy, that evil green-eyed monster. They were willing to kill Anna for their own advancement. Perhaps there was even more at stake with the control of the Five Hundred and the global economy.

Ruby didn't have any more time. Instinctively her fingers found the settings she needed on the rocket pack controls and soon she was flying toward the meadow at top speed. Normally these duels were conducted at a high altitude and out in the countryside so no spectators would be hurt. This place wasn't ideal, but her sister and niece had given her little choice.

Ruby landed next to Anna and looked at her daughter. She hated to do this and hoped Anna wouldn't be embarrassed, but it was her life she was trying to protect.

"Anna, thank you for standing in for me and the War Eagles, but I think I can take it from here. Maybe you can help me with another problem, okay?" She saw a look of concern cross Anna's face.

"Certainly, Mom, if you feel up to it. I relinquish the challenge to you," Anna said calmly before she turned off her rocket pack.

"No problem, Anna. While I take care of this, why don't you get the Speaker and the Parliamentarian as witnesses to this challenge? That way they can make a record of it."

Anna's shoulders visibly relaxed. She smiled at her mother before pulling out her cell phone to make the call.

"Shannon, I answer your challenge and take over for my Champion. Shall we begin in ten minutes?" asked Ruby as she floated again in the air close to Shannon and Marana, then gently set herself on the soft grass near them.

Shannon was having a heated discussion with Marana and Marana was getting angry.

"You can't do that!" yelled Shannon, her eyes blazing with fury. "I challenged Anna, not you. Anna stepped in as your Champion."

Ruby could now see what had happened. Marana had convinced Shannon that she would go up against someone who had no idea how to operate a rocket pack, never mind fight with one. But Shannon and Marana knew that Ruby was very good with a rocket pack and was an excellent fighter.

"Shannon, you actually challenged the leader of the Atlanteans, and that would be me. Anna was my Champion, but I am going to fight myself, so the Challenge is mine. Come on now, are we going to fight or are you going to forfeit the challenge —forever?"

Ruby spoke with an amplified, booming voice and smiled as she saw the Speaker and Parliamentarian had arrived, standing on the rise overlooking the vast meadow, watching.

Ruby shifted her gaze back at Shannon in time to see Marana deliver an open-handed slap across her daughter's face. Ruby stopped herself from interfering with the mother and daughter, at least for now.

Ruby saw Shannon turn off her rocket pack and turn to face her, eyes focused on her feet. "I concede the challenge. You are the leader of the Atlanteans by heredity and valor."

Ruby nodded and looked at the Speaker. "Have you witnessed?"

He answered, "We have. The challenge has been met and will be recorded."

Ruby nodded as Anna flew to her and landed at her side.

"Grandmother always said 'if you need to fight or go to war rather than peaceful discussion, you have already lost.' Today we solved our differences peacefully."

Ruby smiled at her daughter. "Your grandmother was correct. The forces of war have been stopped. For now."

A Simple Assignment
Russ Crossley

Cheerful Baby Vickers, known to her clients and her enemies as C.B. Vickers, stared at the computer screen on the cigarette scarred oak desk in her dimly lit office. Her office was on the top floor of a sixty-year-old three-store brick walk-up in the seedy part of town, known more commonly as the wrong side of the tracks.

The message on the screen was from headquarters and it didn't make the digestion of the baloney and cheese on white bread she ate for lunch any easier. "I shouldn't have asked for the extra mayo," she muttered under her breath as she read the message.

Being a private eye in Degenerate City, which was brimming with the human flotsam, who lived perpetually on the naughty list, had seemed a fairly simple assignment. Every December she reconfirmed the name's of many of the city residents whose appearance on the naughty list remained valid. Alternately she confirmed if any had died by gunshot, suicide, or drug overdose and thus were no longer eligible for any list either nice or naughty.

But every now and then a request came in she dreaded because it usually involved an individual she first recommended be put on the naughty list, and that he or she had moved to the city. A city where she was responsible to clean up the mean streets and sweep away the trash. Now she would have to find him and confirm he hadn't reformed from his naughty ways. Indigestion swelled from the pit of her stomach sending a taste of unprocessed sandwich mingled with the acid of bile to the back of her throat. She swallowed to calm her innards.

The oak captains chair creaked in the quiet as she stood and used her hands to smooth the fabric of her pantsuit jacket. She walked to the wooden coat tree across the office her leather heels clicking on the ancient tiles. She first snagged the fedora hanging off the tree then relieved from one of the ornately carved hooks on the ring surrounding the top of the rack her tanned knee length trench coat. With practiced ease she placed the hat atop her nest of shiny black hair styled into a neat bun atop her oval shaped head. The felt hat tipped as it sat at just the right angle—the way she preferred to wear it—exposing a single pointed ear.

She then slipped her slender, muscular arms into the coat and quickly buttoned it then tied the belt careful to ensure the shoulder holster under her tailored jacket was still easy to access should she need it. The Colt Mustang Lite pistol provided her with the stopping power she had needed on several occasions in dark alleys when cornering suspects. The local PD never complained when she ventilated a few of their most wanted.

Vickers opened her office door into the reception area where their executive assistant Tela Bunster sat at her desk staring at the computer screen. The red head wore a form fitting paisley dress and black horn rimmed glasses perched near the tip of her perfectly shaped up turned nose. Her green eyes shifted to Vickers as she entered the outer office and shut her office door behind her.

"Hey, Vickers," Tela greeted her in her always cheerful voice.

"Hey, Tela, where's Sam?" Vickers and Smooth Sammy Smith had been partners as Private Investigators ever since she moved to the city fifteen years ago.

Tela shrugged. "Last he told me he was tailing a suspect on the other side of the tracks."

Vickers smiled to herself. The suspect was probably female and probably had more than a few coins in her expensive jeans. The other side of the tracks was where money went to live like real people. "Okay, I'm off to see the Lieutenant at HQ downtown. Then I'll probably be out of the office for the next two days. If anything important comes up call me on my cell. Otherwise take names and numbers and tell them me or Sammy will follow up later."

"Sure, boss lady." She smiled warmly then went back to staring at her computer screen.

Tela exited the main office into the corridor beyond closing the door behind her. She pulled her cell phone from her left jacket pocket and touched the quick dial number for Lieutenant Jack

Spike O'Malley's direct line then headed for the stairs. The line buzzed twice then a man answered whose voice she didn't recognize. "Degenerate Police. Sargent Mons speaking."

"Hey, Sarge," she said as reached the head of the wide staircase. "This is C.B. Vickers. I'm lookin' for Lieutenant O'Malley."

"Yeah, Vickers. Right." He sounded uncertain as if unsure how to respond which wasn't a good sign. "Ummm, the Captain wants ta talk to you."

"Is everything okay?"

"Sorry, Vickers, you have to ask to the Cap'n."

Vickers considered her options for a second or two then said, "Okay, tell her I'll be there in fifteen." She ended the call before the Sargent could respond.

When she reached the bottom of the stairs she thumbed the Uber icon on her phone to ordering a car. Her stomach knotted as she waited. Captain Ramona Padds and her didn't get along as well as she did with the Lieutenant, but since Vickers had helped Jack close a number of big outstanding cases these past few years Padds had grown from pure hatred to tolerating what she characterized as interference by a rent-a-cop. In street vernacular rent-a-cop means security officer, but Vickers wasn't about to correct Padds misuse of street lingo. She needed the Cap 'n's approval to continue Spike O'Malley's cooperation, at least in the open. And Vickers wasn't about to be responsible for O'Malley getting fired just for associating with a PI. Never mind the fact she needed him to continue providing her inside information about her investigations as he had these past years. He made her assignments really simple.

She stepped out onto the sidewalk. The scent of damp rotting garbage made from the incessant rain they'd had lately filled her senses. The street lamp at the corner flickered and would soon burn out. A gray four-door sedan appeared at the corner. She noted the man behind the wheel was black. He nodded at her then came around the corner and pulled up beside her.

Leaning across the bench seat he rolled down the passenger side window. "Uber, lady?"

"Yeah." She moved to the rear door and opened it then stepped in and sat eyeing the driver. Uber employed a mixed bag of drivers from high school kids to retirees on a fixed income struggling to keep up with inflation. This guy was wearing a brown leather coat and was cleaned shaven. His broad shoulders and strong hands made her hesitant. He didn't seem like the usual type to be driving a ride share. She mentally shrugged. Who was she to judge a book by its cover?

She slammed the door shut with a bang. "Where we goin'?" asked the driver still faced forward his dark eyes staring at her in the rear view mirror.

"Police HQ. You know the place?"

The driver chuckled. "Nice try, lady. Strap yourself in and we're off."

The car pulled away from the curb the headlights cutting the dark, wet streets like twin golden spears. Vickers smiled to herself. A member of the scum club would instinctively deny any knowledge of the cop shop.

Her eyes narrowed when the driver made a turn she didn't expect. She decided to wait a while before saying anything. In her experience the wise guys could be touchy about a critique. So far this guy was an unknown. He could be just a bad driver.

Slipping her hand into her suit jacket she unbuttoned the strap securing her pistol in the holster. No point taking any chances.

The driver took a street she knew was headed away from Police HQ. "Driver, where are we going?"

Suddenly a wall of glass rose from a slot in the bench seat in front of her cutting her off from the driver. Her heart skipped a beat. She pulled her pistol and flicked off the safety. "Pull over," she growled.

"Take it easy, lady." The driver's voice came from hidden speakers. "The windows and that glass divider between us are bullet proof, and the front seat is reinforced with Kevlar." With her free hand Vickers tested the door handle. As she suspected it was locked.

If she fired her pistol the bullets would bounce around the car and she could end up wounding or even killing herself. Sighing she reengaged the guns safety then shoved it back in the holster. "Okay, but I need to know where you're taking me." She arched an eyebrow. "And it better not be any funny business."

The driver snorted derisively. "You're not my type, lady. Elves are not my thing." She saw him grinning at her in the rearview mirror. "The boss wants ta see you."

"About what?"

He shook his head. "I don't ask the boss for reasons. I like breathin'."

Vickers nodded and leaned back against the seat. Her heart rate slowed as the shot of adrenaline was consumed by her system. She crossed her arms and turned her attention to the streets they were taking. *We must be headed for city hall.* The city's boss of all bosses had granted her an audience, the first time since she moved to the city. She had to wonder why the mayor wanted to see her. *Could it be connected to the message from North Pole Operations?*

Her eyes narrowed. If these events were connected then what seemed at first a routine case had taken on a more deadly and more urgent air. "Not good," she muttered under her breath.

———

The Uber stopped outside an abandoned warehouse on the pier

where mule ships dropped off their contraband. A single street-light cast a soft glow over the gray steel building whose doors she noticed were closed. The fog had begun rolling in washing over the pier and the expansive dock that disappeared into the darkness beyond the grasp of light from the street lamp. The billowing fog gave everything a slightly hazy, fuzzed out appearance.

She swung the car door open after paying the driver and stepped onto the cracked pavement. The smells of age and salty sea air assaulted her senses.

The driver should have dropped her at city hall, but he assured her this was where he'd been instructed to take her. Eying, with one eyebrow arched, the twin doors of the warehouse she swallowed hard to steady her nerves. She pulled out her pistol flipping off the safety once the weapon was freed of the leather holster. She wasn't about to enter the building without adequate protection.

"I should have brought a howitzer," she muttered.

Looking both ways she stepped toward the doors and stopped her heart beating suddenly faster as one of the doors began to open outward on shrill rusty hinges.

A tall, massive figure wearing an ankle length oil black trench coat appeared from the darkness beyond the warehouse doors. He wore scuffed brown leather shoes and a wide brimmed fedora that hid his features.

He spied her and began to walk toward her his arms were the size of tree trunks and he moved like a glacier seemingly getting larger with each step. Her hand gripped the handle of the pistol hanging at her side as she watched him begin to blot out what little light there was from the street lamp behind him that seemed to becoming dimmer with each passing second.

Stopping in front of her he said in a gravel cruncher of a voice, "You Vickers?" She nodded her eyes flitting back and forth across his wide frame.

He turned his back to her. "Follow me." Without another word he began to walk away from her toward the warehouse. Keeping her pistol handy she followed after the giant, her eyes studying her surroundings. Obviously the mayor wasn't the boss she'd expected to be summoned to see. So who was the mysterious boss? She knew all of the bosses in the city and the Uber driver hadn't been one of the local's minions who usually came to see her when one of them wanted her for some borderline illegal purpose. Sometimes the legality wasn't as borderline as other times.

Once inside the warehouse she continued to follow the giant into the dimly lit interior. There was some flickering from overhead lights hanging from the metal roof far above that cast limited illumination over the vast warehouse. She could see delivery trucks lined up parked down one side of the long warehouse floor. Opposite these vehicles were metal shelves that extended to a few feet from the ceiling. Long wooden boxes were stacked on the shelves.

In the distance she saw a grouping of offices with large windows providing unobstructed views of the entire warehouse.

The sound of their footsteps echoed around them and the unpleasant odor of gas and oil filled Vickers nostrils making her already tense stomach want to rebel.

A dark skinned man appeared from the interior of the office exiting through a side door. He wore a shoulder holster over a vest obviously part of a three-piece suit. The gun in the holster looked more like a cannon than small arms. Vickers put away her comparative peashooter and swallowed hard. She was definitely out gunned.

The man's shiny black hair was slicked back on his oval shaped head and a cigarette dangling from his lips. "You Vickers?" he asked. Again she nodded.

The right side of his small mouth curled up in a sly grin. "Great. We've been expectin' ya. Com'on in." His coal black eyes shifted to the mountain. "Get somethin' ta eat, Gus. I'll call ya if we need ya." The big man grunted and walked away.

The slick man smiled weakly at her and ushered her into the offices. She walked past him and he followed her inside. "Name's Parker, Al Parker. I'm the boss's right hand."

Looking around the dilapidated office crowded with old metal desks upon which were stacks of paper, forms and brown glass ashtrays filled to the brim with spent butts.

"Over there in the back," said Al as he waved her to the rear of the office where there was a scarred wood door with a fogged glass window. In the center of the window in black block letters was the word, PRIVATE. Al cut in front of her and opened the door then ushered her inside.

Stepping inside the small office Vickers saw a strawberry blonde woman seated behind a desk that had seen better days in the 1940's. She wore a mottled gray crew neck short-sleeved tee shirt and was smoking a cigarette. She looked up from her laptop screen when Vickers walked in. Parker walked away leaving the door open.

"Take a seat, detective," said her voice low and menacing. Her emerald green eyes followed Vickers as she crossed the office to sit in one of the two oak captains chairs in front of the desk. Removing her fedora she allowed her hair to cascade about her shoulders. Dropping the hat into the matching chair she cast her gaze about the shabby room.

Two walls were composed of frame glass panes providing the person seated at the desk a good view of the office and the warehouse beyond. Behind the desk was a wall of battered army green file cabinets. There were no pictures on the wall over the cabinets nor was there a picture frame on the desk only in and out baskets and files stacked to the red heads right. The room smelled of age, mould and stale tobacco.

The woman placed the pen in her right hand on the desk next

to the laptop and eased back against the low-slung executive chair. She offered Vickers a wry humorless smile.

"Well, if it isn't Cheerful Baby Vickers."

"C.B.," Vickers corrected her.

The woman laughed followed by a shrug of her narrow shoulders. "As you wish, C.B." She stood and walked to the office door, which she closed. "It's not often I have an Elf in my office. One of Santa's finest." She sat back down in the chair across from Vickers and arched one reddish eyebrow. "My name's Ophelia Wrecker. President of Wrecker Toys."

Vickers studied Ophelia looking for any signs of deception. Seeing none she said, "What happened to Laertes?" She knew the answer but wanted to know if this woman was the real thing.

Ophelia's attempt at easy humor evaporated like raindrops on a summer day. She looked away before responding. "I think you know perfectly well, but as you know he's returned to town recently and has contacted me..." her words dropped away.

Sitting upright in her chair Ophelia reached to her right out, of Vickers view, which made Vickers heart rate spike. Instinctively her hand slipped inside her trench coat her fingers grasping the butt of her pistol.

The sound of a drawer opening made Vickers breath catch in her throat. She didn't want to shoot Wrecker unless absolutely necessary. Wrecker Toys had been connected to the North Pole operation for decades and killing the matriarch of the world's biggest toy conglomerate would be bad for business. And the big boss would be very unhappy.

Ophelia's hand reappeared her fingers grasping a manila envelope. Vickers pulled her hand from inside her coat releasing her pistol and her heart rate decreased dramatically. Never assume the worst, she scolded herself. Jumping to conclusions was definitely her worst trait.

"I have information compiled by my corporate spy division about my brother you may find useful in locating him."

Vickers frowned at the toy company executive. "I thought he was in the city."

She shrugged in response. "It's a big city."

Vickers realized what was going on here. "Your people haven't been able to find him?" She shook her head. "And you want me to find him so your thugs can rub him out." She eyed Ophelia looking for a reaction. When there was none she continued. "Why me?

Ophelia avoided Vickers steady gaze. "You put his name on the naughty list." Her cheeks flushed with color. "There have been rumors."

Vickers chuckled. "Rumors? Com'on, Ophelia, your brother's a criminal. He and I only shared a pair of handcuffs until I delivered him to the police station. He deserved to be on the list."

Once again Ophelia arched an eyebrow. "And now?"

"That's what I've been asked to investigate."

"Why?"

Vickers hesitated. She had no idea why she was asked to investigate anyone, ever. It was her job. Head office sent her the names to her by e-mail and she investigated. Each month they paid her for each closed investigation and that was it. A simple assignment.

"Why're you so interested anyway?"

Ophelia visibly relaxed and eased back in her chair back causing the ancient chair to creak loudly. "I should have known better than to think I could hide anything from a gumshoe." She sighed. "Laertes plans to take over the family business," she explained, "and I'm told he plans to change our entire inventory and manufacturing process."

"To what?" Wrecker toys had been manufacturing the same way for over a hundred years. The North Pole operation was dependent on their steady supply every delivery season.

Ophelia's forehead wrinkled and her eyebrows fell into a deep scowl. Her voice sank to a growl. "He wants to make toys that don't break in the first two days of the kids getting their grubby paws on them."

———

According to the file Ophelia Wrecker provided Vickers first stop would be the bus station. Like any city the bus station was located in the seediest part of the already seediest part of town. In Degenerate the bus station was located next to the police headquarters. This made it convenient for the cops when the latest round of recent parolees arrived in town. The cops would shake them down to ensure they knew to be good boys and girls when the hit the streets. It also helped the cops to line their pockets with bribe money since the former inmates had been loaded on the bus with some of their home states tax money to start their new life of freedom. Skimming half the proceeds was considered arrival tax. If they refused to pay they would be turned around and sent back to prison on some trumped up parole violation.

The system was illegal but highly effective so the upper police brass looked the other way. Of course it also meant they were all on the naughty list. But most of them had been on the list since before they were ten years of age.

The Uber stopped near the terminal entrance and Vickers got out. Ophelia had prepaid the driver so without a word the driver drove away leaving her standing amid the hustle and bustle of people entering and exiting the terminal doors. She froze when she spotted Spike O'Malley standing to the left of the twin glass doors smoking a cigarette in his ill-fitting cop suit and unpolished black leather shoes. His handsome chiseled features were blank his dark eyes staring at her. Spike was seriously pissed and she had a sinking feeling she knew why.

Walking up to him she spoke first. "How's Captain Padds?"

"Mad." He shrugged. "No, furious...yes, furious is a much better description."

"Not surprising, but I have an alibi."

He smirked and stubbed out the remainder of his cigarette in the large ashtray next to him. "You always do."

"So why're you here?" He opened his mouth to speak but she cut him off. "To snatch me to deliver to the captain?" He shook his head slowly keeping his eyes on her.

"Ah, yes, of course." She pursed her lips. "To keep an eagle eye on my investigation." He offered a humorless smile in response and nodded.

"Good. Let's go inside and get started." Stuffing his hands in his suit pants pockets he followed her inside the terminal. A wall of stale grease, urine, and rancid smoke, born from decades of abuse to the building, greeted them.

Ignoring the accumulated odors of decades of city life she strode toward the sign affixed high up near the ceiling across terminal signaling the offices were located under it. Due to the crowded seating area her view was obstructed by people milling about chatting, children running and shouting and porters moving trollies about stacked high with voluminous luggage and boxes. Thankfully no one appeared to be paying attention to them as they weaved their way through the sea of humanity.

A woman's scream made everyone freeze in place and the crowd parted as she appeared from the back of the building looking frantic, eyes wild with fear and blood on one hand. "Help! Murder...murder...come quick..." She turned away and started running toward the rear exit through the wide gap in the crowd she had created with her screaming.

Glancing at Spike Vickers pulled her pistol as he pulled his 1911 automatic from the shoulder holster hidden by his raincoat and suit jacket. He offered her a sharp nod and together they hurried to follow the woman.

They exited through the rear doors of the terminal their guns ready for the unexpected. But all they found was a collection of steel trash cans scattered like bowling pins across the delivery area to the bus terminal and the staff parking lot beyond. The screaming woman with blood on her right hand stood among a collection of five cans scattered in a semicircle shape waving them over her eyes wild. It was then Vickers noticed her dress was stained with blood as well.

Vickers signaled to Spike with a nod of her head to take the right while she approached the potential scene of the crime from the left. They carefully made there way to where the woman squatted, her eyes were wild with panic that was growing exponentially.

As she got closer Vickers realized she could see the leg of a blood soaked corpse spread-eagled on its back. With each step it dawned on her the killer had long ago departed stage left leaving the victim and the panic stricken woman. She holstered her weapon as the man lying on the ground between the toppled trashcans became fully visible. His blue eyes stared into infinity and his mouth hung open.

"My husband," wailed the distraught woman tears rolling down her pale cheeks.

"Oh, you've got to be kidding," Spike said as he appeared beside her.

"What?" she said, turning to face the detective.

"That's the bus terminal manager, the guy we needed ta talk to."

"How do you know I wanted to talk to him?" She stared at him. "And who said anything about we?"

Spike walked up to the woman. "Who're you again?"

"This is...I mean was my husband...he's been murdered..."

"I got that part. Do you have access to the records your late husband kept?"

Vickers pulled on Spikes arm to drag him away from the woman whose eyes were now wide with horror. "Spike, stop. She's upset. We need to be more sensitive...call the ME." He didn't resist and as he moved away pulled out his cell phone to make the call to the state medical examiner.

"You make the call," Vickers suggested, "while I stay with her."

"What's wrong with him?" the woman complained to Vickers.

"I'm so sorry," she said. "He's a jaded detective who's seen a lot of dead bodies in his career." The woman dropped her arms to her sides and began to sob. Vickers reached out to grab her by the arms just as she began to collapse and eased her to the pavement.

After an hour of consoling the woman and the arrival of the ME and the crime scene techs they ended up sitting in the late managers office with Vickers holding the woman's hands in hers— a tech provided wipes so the woman could wipe off her husbands blood from her hands—half listening to the story of the couples lives and how they ended up in Degenerate City. Vickers spent the time wondering why anyone would kill a bus terminal manager with a life of boredom with this dullest of dull women. The woman was like a bar of old soap. The victims name was Ivan Bluster and her name was Pearl. Not that it mattered to Vickers.

According to Spike who stepped in momentarily to suggest a coffee run—and was soundly rejected by Pearl—Ivan had been stabbed in the heart. From this tidbit of information Vickers knew his death was quick and the murderer was strong. It wasn't easy to run a knife through breastbone. The man mountain that worked for the would-be Princess Wrecker popped into her thoughts, but it didn't make sense for Ophelia Wrecker to whack the guy. She'd sent them to see him in order to locate her brother.

"Did Ivan have any enemies?"

Vickers could see the wheels turning behind Pearl's eyes as she considered the question. Her eyes shifted away from Vickers before she responded. "Yeah, of course." She shrugged. "We get a lot of low life through here and sometimes Ivan had to be tough."

Vickers nodded. "I understand." She understood tough. "Anyone specific?"

Pearl sighed and stood and stepped up to a gray filing cabinet against the wall behind her chair. She opened a drawer and pulled out a file folder overflowing with paper. Closing the drawer she turned back and dropped the folder on the desk and sat back down.

Vickers had to hold back a sneeze when the accumulated dust filled her nostrils. "What is this?"

"Ivan's threat file."

Vickers opened the file and saw there were sheets of papers covered in cut of letters glued to each sheet inside. Lots of 'em. "How many are there in here?"

Pearl shrugged. "I don't know exactly, but probably a hundred or so. I should add these are the ones he received in the past three months." Avoiding Vickers gaze she added, "He used to throw 'em away..." She snorted. "Tough guy."

Vickers picked up the top one. "Pay or you die," she murmured. Putting the note aside she picked up the second one on the stack. "Keep your promise or you'll regret it."

Setting the second one on top of the first she fanned through the remainder of the pile until she came to the second to last of the notes and her eyes went wide. It read, I'm coming to get you. Soon. The she looked at the last one and froze. Tomorrow you die.

Waving the last note in Pearl's direction, "When did Ivan receive this?"

Pearl's voice dropped to a whisper. "Yesterday."

"Hey, Spike, get in here!"

The door opened and Spike appeared. He must have been

listening just outside the door. "What's goin' on, C.B.?" He closed the office door after him.

"I want you here to hear this. Pearl, how did this note arrive? Mail or hand delivered?"

Her brow wrinkled. "I think someone delivered it..." her eyes widened. "A delivery service." The creases on her pale forehead grew deeper. "Maximum...something."

"Spike?" Vickers said looking to O'Malley.

"Maximum Speed. I know them. Twenty-four hour a day operation. Their head office is downtown. Bleeker at 4th Ave."

"Then I guess we have our next breadcrumb."

———

The unmarked dusky blue police car Spike had checked out of the motor pool stopped next to the curb outside the headquarters of Maximum Speed Delivery. The company name was arrayed across the front of the soot covered brick building ten story building in large red neon letters.

Through the large display windows facing the street Vickers could see several employees dressed in matching blue jumpsuits the company logo emblazoned across the chest in the shape of a lightning bolt. They were busily moving packaging and letters to a conveyor belt sticking from hole a wall at the rear of the office. Given the configuration of the lobby within the large building there must be a sorting warehouse located at the other end of the belt behind the wall. In front of the belt was a long service counter with several stations to accept packages and letters from customers. There were a few customers dropping boxes and envelopes off and a couple picking up at one end of the counter.

"What was that name again?" asked Vickers.

"Mox. Albert Mox. The manager," replied Spike his dark eyes

narrowing as he studied the interior of the delivery company office as if looking for this Mox character.

Vickers studied the staff visible through the window. The tall, black man would be her guess, though it could be any male. The black man appeared confident and his uniform was pressed and neat. His shoes were polished and appeared new.

"Ah, there." Spike broke Vickers introspection when he pointed at a woman entering the office from a door leading to the warehouse beyond. "Good. I was worried Albert might not be on shift this time of night."

Albert's a woman? Vickers shrugged. Why not?

They entered through the glass front door causing a sensor to ring a bell alerting the staff that a potential customer had entered. Vickers smiled to herself. Conditioned responses worked every time. Even at the North Pole operation where Mr. C was very fond of the idea. Of course this was why she had been assigned this job. Automaton was not in her job description.

"Hey, Albert," said Spike as if greeting an old friend.

For her part Mox arched an eyebrow at him and her brow wrinkled as a deep scowl formed on her smooth forehead. Her milk chocolate complexion and dark eyes betrayed her beauty beneath the coverall uniform and the ponytail trailing down her back between her shoulder blades. Spike certainly seemed smitten.

His eyes were wide like a new puppy and he seemed unusually nervous for an experienced homicide detective. "You okay, big guy? Vickers asked.

He shifted his gaze to her and scowled. "Yeah. Why?"

"Nothing. You seemed nervous."

"I'm not," he barked in a whispered tone as they came with hearing range of the delivery company manager.

"Well if it isn't O'Malley the big shot cop," Mox said in a sarcastic tone her arms crossed over her chest a smirk on her lips.

"Perhaps we should retire to your office?" suggested Spike.

Mox regarded him silently for several seconds. "Okay, let's go." She dropped her arms to her sides. "But it changes nothing."

Spike raised his hands in mock surrender. "Lead on, boss lady."

Mox snorted derisively as she turned round and led the way to the door to the warehouse. Soon they were standing in her office on one corner of the warehouse the door closed and the blinds pulled down tight.

Vickers eyes flitted between the two adversaries wondering what would happen next.

Without warning Mox strode up to stand in front of Spike then wrapped her arms around him and pressed her lips firmly to his. They maintained this position for several seconds until they finally parted. She grinned salaciously. "Hi there, Spikey, been far too long."

His cheeks flushed red. "Yeah, sorry, Alley. I've been working like a whipped dog. The Cap'n seems to think I can close a lot of the open cases."

"Who's the skirt?" She eyed Vickers.

"Alley Mox meet C.B. Vickers. The best PI in town."

"Nice ears," Mox said nodding a greeting at Vickers who offered a mirthless smile in return. "What's C.B. stand for?"

Vickers grunted humorlessly. "Whatever you wish." Mox laughed breaking through Vickers shield of instant distrust. "Spike and I are investigatin' a murder. We need your help."

Alley Mox stopped laughing and her eyes narrowed and her lips formed a thin line. "You know we need to see a warrant to show you anything?" she said.

Vickers was stunned how quickly Mox became all business. Few people could shift from humor to serious so quickly. Vickers would be on guard with this woman. She was formable and should not be underestimated.

"Of course, Alley," said Spike. His eyes shifted to Vickers. "We know the rules. What we're looking for is someone who dropped off sealed envelopes addressed to the bus terminal manager."

Mox's eyes flitted between them then her expression softened. She had crossed her arms again. "Is that who's dead?" Knowing Spike wouldn't say so he'd maintain the integrity of the investigation Vickers nodded. Mox arched an eyebrow in response. "Makes sense...looking back I mean."

Vickers jumped all over the delivery company manager's words. "What makes sense?"

"The envelopes were dropped off here by a kid in prepaid envelopes."

"Do you know this kid?" asked Spike.

"Ya know I hadn't put it together until just now," replied Mox seemingly distracted. "As soon as you said Ivan was dead I knew it..." She closed her eyes and her chin sunk to her chest.

"Knew what?" Vickers said softly.

"Ivan was a friend. He helped me get this job when I hit town..."

"You're on the naughty list. Right?"

Mox's lips formed a sly smile and her eyes shifted toward Spike. "The very naughty list actually." Spike flushed from his neck to the top of his forehead and the tips of his ears.

Vickers grunted and rolled her eyes. "I would hose you two down with cold water right now, but we have pressing business." She glared at Spike who avoided her by looking away. "We have a murderer to catch." Vickers shifted her attention to Mox. "So who is this kid?"

"He's a newspaper boy who hawks his wares over on the corner of Dalmatian and Halveron."

"How many times has he made drop offs?"

Mox shrugged. "I personally have seen him drop off envelopes once a week for the past three months. Always the same day, always around the same time." Her brow wrinkled. "But not this week," she murmured as her frown deepened. "Now I know why."

"The name?" asked Spike having managed to regain his composure.

Mox seemed to wake up. "Sorry, it's just when a friend is killed it affects you. Ya know?" Vickers eyes shifted to Spike whose outward appearance of the hard-as-steel detective had disappeared replaced by a man of compassion. He nodded and placed a comforting hand on Mox's shoulder his eyes dropping. She wanted to wretch at the display of emotion but held back.

"I get it, Alley," Vickers said, "but we need to talk to this boy before our trail grows cold."

Mox swiped her eyes with the back of one hand. "Of course. His name is Sydney Bottom." Her eyes suddenly glared as anger flushed her cheeks. "The bastard that did this needs to pay for Ivan's death."

"We will do our best," said Vickers grabbing Spike by his arm and dragging him toward the office door. "Right, Spike?"

"Yes, of course," he said, his eyes wide with wonder. Her dramatic mood swings had finally drawn his attention.

They soon were seated in his unmarked police car the only sound the low murmured to the police radio calls as background noise. "What the heck was that all about?" Vickers said breaking the silence.

Spike shrugged. "I slept with her a couple of times."

Vickers rolled her eyes. "Of course you did." She shook her head and grunted derisively. "Never mind, let's go. We need to find this kid."

Spike nodded his eyes focused on the road and started the car. There wasn't a lot of traffic this time of day so he quickly pulled away from the curb and they headed for their next breadcrumb in this chase to find the killer of Ivan Bluster. Her priority was finding Laertes Wrecker to confirm he should remain on the naughty list. This murder stuff was becoming a distraction from her official assignment.

———

They arrived at the corner of Dalmatian and Halveron to find no sign of Sydney Bottom. Vickers checked her watch and saw the late edition of the paper was due out an hour. They would have to wait.

"Park over there," she said, pointing to an empty parking spot at the corner on Halverson where they would have a good view of the paperboy's corner office.

The engine noise died away replaced by the sound of rain striking the roof of the unmarked police car. Vickers scanned the area not sure exactly what she was looking for. She finally landed on a large dark car with blacked out windows. The mystery car was parked on Dalmatian about four spaces from the corner. Unable to see if anyone was inside Vickers grew suspicious and her stomach tightened.

"How 'bout I get us a coupla of tuna fish subs from Max's? I know I could eat," Spike said, slumping in the drivers seat beside her.

"I'm hungry too, but I think it will have to wait a while longer." She tapped his shoulder and directed his attention to the large car.

He peered at the mystery car his eyes slits. "What? It's a big black car. What's the big deal?"

"One of our last leads was murdered?"

Sighing Spike opened the car door and stepped out onto the sidewalk. Vickers did the same. "Okay, let's check it out. You may be right."

They looked both ways then crossed the street just after a taxi drove past. Spike pulled his weapon and nodded to Vickers to split away to watch his flank. They approached the car from opposite directions until Spike was beside the driver's side door. He shifted his gun to his left hand and rapped his knuckles on the window.

Accompanied by a soft whirr the window came down revealing a large man with a black goatee and a baldhead. He glared at Spike. "What ya want, cop?"

Spike wasn't actually sure why but he forged ahead. "Why are you parked here?"

"What's it to ya?" growled the driver in his husky voice.

To Vickers dismay Spike holstered his gun. "We're here to meet someone and we have to make sure no one's going to interfere."

"Tell me sumthin' that's my problem," said the driver before closing the window.

Vickers looked to her left and saw the newsboy walking toward the street corner. It had to be him he had two large pouch-like bags the straps crisscrossed over his chest. He was taller than she expected, but freckle faced and carrot red hair sticking from under his backward facing baseball cap made him about as clichéd as you expect for a newsboy.

"He's here, Spike. Let's go talk to him."

Spike shrugged. "Yeah, I guess so. These guys seem harmless enough."

Vickers arched an eyebrow at the detective. Some days she really wondered how he had earned his badge, and how he kept it.

They left the large car and started to walk toward the kid. After they were a few yards away Vickers stole a quick glance over her shoulder. The rear seat window was coming down and she could see the barrel of a semi automatic rifle coming from inside the darkness-shrouded interior.

"Gun!" She dropped to her belly onto the pavement as did

Spike. Her eyes flitted to the kid. He was still a few dozen yards away, but rather than dropping to the ground he froze his eyes wide with fear. She and Spike rolled onto their backs and after pulling their guns out fired repeatedly at the shooter in the passenger side window. The cars powerful engine roared to life and as the rear window slid closed it began to pull away. Vickers closed one eye and aimed at the front right tire before firing two quick shots.

There was a loud thump as the tire was hit and the car swerved out of control. It struck a lamppost the hood crushed like an accordion by the impact and thick black smoke pouring from the engine.

Vickers rose slowly to her feet keeping her pistol trained on the car watching to see if the gunman would appear. Spike was up as well and stood to her left his pistol too trained on the wreck. They moved slowly forward keeping abreast of each other.

"Vickers, you better check on the kid," Spike said, "I'll take care of these creeps."

Vickers glanced back over her shoulder and spotted the newsboy lying on his back not moving. She nodded to Spike then turned and ran to the kid's side keeping her gun at the ready just in case a second shooter appeared. The side of his head had a bloody gash where a bullet had grazed him and his left leg was lying in a pool of blood. Kneeling beside him, Vickers pulled off the belt of her trench coat and used to make a tourniquet for his bleeding leg. She then pulled out her cell phone and called 911 to get an ambulance. At least he was still breathing.

The kid and their only lead were both out cold.

———

They'd been at the hospital for four hours drinking stale coffee bathed in the antiseptic smells of what had to be the cleanest building in the city. Finally a doctor dressed in green scrubs approached them. His ruddy features were marked by fatigue and there were the beginnings of shadows under his blue eyes.

"Are you Detective O'Malley?" he said to Spike.

"Yes." Spike accepted his offer of a handshake. "How's the kid?"

The doctor's eyes dropped to avoid looking Spike in the eyes. "He's not out of the woods yet, but we managed to stem the bleeding. The bullet in his left leg cut a major artery. Thankfully the makeshift tourniquet saved his life. The bullet went through without hitting bone which also helped."

"What's the prognosis?" Vickers asked, after dropping her empty Styrofoam coffee cup in the near to overflowing trash can next to the leatherette waiting room couch.

The doctor looked uncertain for a couple of seconds. "It's early, but I think he'll survive."

"Can we talk to him?"

"He's heavily medicated, but I know you need to speak to him as soon as possible. If I let you see him for a minute or two would that be okay?"

Spike's cell rang. He pulled it out and opened the connection. "Yeah?" He listened intently for a few seconds then cut the connection and put his phone back in his pocket. "They finally tracked down the registered owner's identity." Before Vickers could ask what the call was about he added, "I'll tell ya after we talk ta the kid."

Vickers wondered why it took so long to run a license plate. The shooter and the driver were dead but they had the car. She followed Spike to the boy's hospital room.

They found him conscious but groggy. Vickers moved a chair to his beside and after sitting placed one hand on his. "Hi," she said softly. A weak smile passed over the boy's lips. "We got the guys that shot you." He nodded he understood. "We need to know who gave you the envelopes to take to Maximum Speed Delivery."

The boy shook his head. He wasn't going to cooperate. Vickers thought for a minute. Ahhhh... "Listen, kid, who ever ordered these guys to kill you is the same person who gave you the envelopes."

The Kid's eyes flitted side to side until a tear ran down one cheek. He brought up one hand and signaled for Vickers to come closer. Vickers brought an ear to closer to his mouth and he whispered to her. She patted his hand softly. "Okay, kid, we'll take care of it. I promise." He nodded then his eyes closed and he began breathing deeply as sleep overcame him.

Once in the hallway Spike asked what the kid said. "You tell me first why it took so long to run that plate number."

Spike arched an eyebrow. "Okay. The plates on the shooters car were stolen. So we had to run the VIN. It took four hours because someone changed the VIN by one number. Once the guys at auto theft figured it out they soon traced the buyer of the car." He paused. "A numbered holding company bought the car three months ago. Now this is normally a dead end until we discovered the sole owner of this particular holding company is Allan Q. Parker. Ophelia Wreckers right hand guy."

Vickers crossed her arms over her chest and snorted, a wry smile formed on her lips. "I know," she said simply.

"How do you know?"

"The kid just whispered to me Al Parker was the one who paid him to deliver the envelopes to Maximum Speed."

———

They arrived at Wrecker Toys with two backup units sirens blaring and lights illuminating the darkness with red and blue flashes.

Spike directed two of the uniformed officers to cover the back of the building while Vickers, he and the other two officers would go in the front. The officers were armed with shotguns and they wore body armor.

Once inside they needed flashlights to find their way through the darkened warehouse. The smell of dust permeated everything. The building appeared deserted. Finally there was a soft glow of light ahead beyond the steel shelving piled high with cardboard boxes.

Once they cleared the last of the shelving they could see Ophelia's office where they'd first met the toy maker. In the subdued lighting of her office they discovered Al Parker with a pistol held to Ophelia's head, his normally handsome features marred by an angry glare. "One step more and she dies," he screamed with spittle shooting from his mouth.

Vickers shot a look at Spike who nodded. They had to hold back until there was an opportunity to take the guy out. Ophelia's eyes were wild with raw fear and beads of perspiration dotted her forehead. Her mouth hung open slightly and she trembled badly.

"You're surrounded," Spike said sternly. "Give up now."

Suddenly a figure stepped out of the darkness to their right and fired a single shot that startled Vickers with its loudness. There was a slight sound of breaking glass then a bloody round hole appeared in the middle of Parkers forehead. His expression sagged into a look of shock as he dropped the gun. It clattered to the floor at his feet. He then slowly collapsed to the floor as if he were a balloon that had sprung leak. Realizing she was free Ophelia leapt to her feet and ran out of the office.

Breathing hard and her breath ragged she bent forward at the waist then vomited as her sudden escape from certain death threatened to overwhelm her. Finally she managed to regain her composure as Spike and the two police officers went to check

Parker and retrieve his pistol. They would secure the scene for the ME.

Vickers turned to the shooter who had holstered his weapon. She eyed him quizzically. He was a tall, well-built man wearing a fedora and a gray double-breasted suit. "Aren't you Laertes Wrecker?"

"Yes," he said, his voice reminding her of the crunch of gravel underfoot.

"I've been looking for you," she said.

He tipped back his hat and arched one dark eyebrow at her. "Really? Why?"

"I work for North Pole operations. My job is to confirm the persons on the naughty list should remain on that list. You are my current investigation."

He chuckled. "Me?" He paused as his eyes narrowed in suspicion. "How did you get involved in this police investigation?"

Vickers winced slightly. "Spike and I are friends. I asked him for help tracking you down. I inadvertently became involved when my only lead was murdered."

Now Laertes laughed. "None of this sounds real to me."

Vickers smiled as the tension she felt dropped away. "I know it sounds ridiculous." She brushed back her hair with her fingers to reveal her elfin ears. "I'm an elf so from my perspective on the realm of the possible is somewhat more vast than most."

Laertes stopped laughing and his expression became serious. "Okay, fine. I have to check on my sister." Vickers nodded then he moved to be beside Ophelia wrapping one around her waist to hold her up.

Vickers stood outside Ophelia's office watching the two officers carefully securing the scene. Spike came up beside her. "What ya think?"

Vickers shrugged. "I think Laertes loves his sister." Spike chuckled grimly.

She would have to e-mail North Pole operations and advise them to move Laertes to the good list. He had not only saved his sister by killing Parker, but probably a few other lives in a potential shootout.

Parker died with no hope of escaping the naughty list. Murder of the bus terminal manager and hiring gunmen to attempt the murder of a young boy were guarantees to perpetual naughty.

———

Vickers sat in front of the computer composing the e-mail. She paused as her office door opened and Sam stepped in. He dropped down in one of the leatherette captain's chairs in front of her desk and sighed. He stank of stale whiskey and two day old perspiration. "Hey, C.B., I heard you had a doozy of a case."

She shook her head. "It was a simple assignment. Ya know the usual."

Sam grunted his eyes shifted to the window over looking the street three stories below. "I heard some newspaper kid was hurt. He gonna make it?"

"Yeah, he'll be okay."

Sam's gaze shifted back to her. "What about Wrecker Toys?"

Why was her partner so interested? "They'll be producing the same garbage as always."

"Good." He nodded. "Well, I gotta go. I have a retainer to earn." He moved to rise from the chair.

She arched an eyebrow at him. "Sam?" Her partner stopped. "Why this sudden interest in Wrecker Toys? You don't have any kids."

"My client is an heir to the Wrecker fortune. If they were to change their business model it might affect her fortune."

And thereby potential wife number nine's fortune, Vickers thought. Sam collected wives like kids collected hockey cards.

"Ophelia Wrecker's brother, Laertes, left town shortly after shooting a guy sent to kill her." She smirked derisively making Sam visibly uncomfortable. He rose from the chair preparing to leave. He'd heard the information he wanted when he entered her office.

"I'll see ya later, Sam. Make sure you close the door on your way out."

He nodded and was quickly out the door slamming it behind him.

A slow smile spread over Vickers lips then quickly faded as she once again began composing her e-mail.

CAPTAIN VIRTUE AND THE LEAGUE
OF EVIL

Russ Crossley

RED increased power to the twin thrusters of the rocket
pack as they approached the dirigible visible through
the thin cloud cover just below them at four thousand
feet.

There was a high probability they were about to experience a
fiery death—well, Virtue would die of course but not RED. The
dangerous high-speed approach was to demonstrate they were not
adverse to use courage, disregard for personal safety, and adapt-
ability when under the pressure of a deadline. They needed this
contract. Badly. Virtue needed to eat and she needed a new
supply of radioactive isotopes.

"Hey, RED, watch it," Virtue said over the comm in his flight
helmet. "Isn't this a little fast?"

"Don't worry, Virtue, trust me."

"Okay," His deep baritone sounded apprehensive, but since

he wasn't the brightest star in the heavens. RED was certain Virtue would do whatever RED told him. More importantly the pilot had signed an unbreakable contract ten years ago. Wherever RED goes so goes Captain Virtue.

The sensors said they were now within fifty yards of the fast moving air ship. The sensors also showed the coordinates of door they would use to enter that ship. RED adjusted their course slightly and prepared for the approach maneuver. Timing must be perfect or the virtual recorders wouldn't have the images he wanted the military brass to see. An exploding rocket pack and a dirigible crashing to the ground entombed in a boiling fireball wouldn't do much for their credibility. Drama is everything when it comes to show biz, RED's father often says. Maybe a little too often but that's a whole other issue in itself.

"We have arrived," said Virtue as they hovered in the air next to the door of the dirigible's passenger·cabin. Three pairs of eyes covered by goggles stared back at them from the windows lining the passenger cabin a look of astonishment on their faces.

Perfect, thought RED. Surprise is an art form when practiced by a virtuoso.

RED transmitted an override signal to unlock the door and prepared to enter the passenger cabin. "Virtue, have your blaster ready."

"Roger wilco."

"Don't use those words, Virtue. We talked about this." Moron. RED rolled her visual receptors as if they were real human eyes.

"Sorry...blaster locked and loaded..." RED made a note to have another talk with Virtue about communication etiquette. This was getting old. Hopefully the potential clients wouldn't notice her partners' faux pas.

The goggled crewmembers of the dirigible had finally sprung into action and were preparing to repel them. RED sensed they were now armed and had their projectile weapons aimed at the door ready for the assault. "Virtue, place a mini bomb on the door." Without thankfully saying anything Virtue took a mini bomb from a sleeve on his utility belt then pressed the magnetized strip located on one side of the small explosive device to the steel door. The wind whipped at his leather flight jacket.

RED activated the rocket pack's maneuvering jets to move them far enough away from the door so the blast wouldn't affect them then triggered the weapon. The bomb blew the door in accompanied by a shower of sparks and a loud thump audible over then the wind. Acrid smoke billowed out from the passenger cabin swept away by the force of the rushing air at this altitude. The twin external rocket engines on the dirigible were still running and Red could register the heat. They needed to avoid going near the exhaust ports of the powerful engines.

"Hold on. We're going in fast. Prepare to fire at any moving target."

"Okay, RED." Virtue responded his tone sharp and focused.

A hint of doubt occurred to RED suggested by previous experience. "Set your weapon on stun, Virtue, we don't need another Toledo." He didn't respond but she knew he understood. The last thing they needed were multiple fatalities as they did in that dead end bar outside the Ohio city when Virtue in a panic fired his weapon into a crowd of angry bikers.

The external sensors had guided them to the perfect spot to enter the smoky interior of the passenger cabin without being in the line of fire of any of the crewmembers inside. If they only have external sensors how do they see what's inside? Confusing Virtue had engaged the infrared feature in his flight helmet and had his blaster out of its holster in his right hand at the ready. RED cut power to the thrusters as they shot through the blasted door of the cabin. The whine power down of the rocket pack's motor echoed in the enclosed space of the cabin after they were shut down.

Once inside one of the crew persons stumbled out of the

smoke in front of them covered head to toe in dark soot. He or she
—the voluminous uniform and leather helmet, plus the goggles
obscuring the eyes, made it impossible to determine the gender—
sagged to the knees and fell forward striking the deck with a loud
slap then lay still. The projectile weapon the crewmember had
been holding skidded across the deck toward them.

"I'm reading two more crew near the flight control panel
straight ahead." Red paused to double check the readings.
"They're out cold. Everyone's alive but unconscious."

"Great," Virtue said proudly holstering his blaster. "Captain
Virtue wins again."

"Really?" RED said sarcastically.

———

After they shut down the dirigibles engines they drifted until two
Navy Special Service dirigibles, plus two F9.9 jet fighters, acting
as escorts, arrived to extract the unconscious crew and retrieve the
payload. Then the enemy dirigible would be towed to the ocean to
be destroyed in a ball of flame by air-to-air missiles. The airships
remains would land in the sea and disappear in the shifting tides.
To hell with the environmentalists, thought RED.

After RED attended a debriefing session without Virtue,
pilots were unnecessary at debriefs, they arrived back at their sixth
floor headquarters—located in an abandoned six story office
building in the middle of a bad part of town—Virtue sighed
wearily then dropped into one the three cigarette scarred oak
chairs in the office. A heavy steel desk sat in the middle of the
room, three of the walls were lined with military gray steel filing
cabinets. The only saving grace was the two open windows facing
the street far below allowed a cool breeze to provide relief from
the odors of mold and rot that filled the room. The breeze was
welcome but the traffic noise rising from the busy street wasn't.

Of course none of this really bothered RED as an AI rocket pack but she did need to provide some creature comforts for her one employee and front man. The contract between them was clear on this point.

Virtue undid the leather strap under his chiseled chin then slipped off his helmet letting it drop to the floor next to the chair with a thump. He then began undoing the buttons of his rust colored leather-flying jacket after he had taken off his heat resistant leather gloves and slapped them on the desk.

"Man, RED, I'm beat. That was a hell of a mission." He ran one hand through his thick, wavy blond hair and closed his eyes as he eased back against the chair back.

"Yeah, I know, kid, but we had to make an impression for the Imperial staff."

Virtue snorted without opening his eyes. He crossed his arms over his wide chest. "What was the payload aboard that dirigible anyway, anything interesting?"

RED made a snort sound that matched Virtue's. "Not that it matters but I'm told it was two crates of fresh pineapples destined for a drug lord on Papaola Island."

"What about the drug lord?" Virtue asked as if he was interested which RED knew he wasn't.

"I don't know they didn't share that detail with me."

"What did they say about our performance?" Virtue responded getting right to the important part of RED's meeting with the brass.

"They liked what they saw but they said they still have us and another team in mind. We seem to be in a tie with LARP and Commander Heroic."

Virtue dropped his arms and his eyes popped open as a scowl spread across his handsome features like a tidal wave. The chair creaked as he sat forward. His azure eyes had an intensity in them RED rarely saw in Virtue. The guy was suddenly lit up by a display of passion something he hadn't displayed in a very long time. What had triggered this did he really want this contract so bad?

"What's up, Virtue? We've been in competition for contracts many times why should this be any different? You're freaking me out."

Before he could respond a delivery truck on the street below ground its gears and began blasting its air horn. This was followed by a prolonged screech of multiple brakes being applied then the impact of metal-on-metal and shattering glass. The cacophony of sound echoing around the small office made conversation impossible.

RED turned her visual interface toward the windows in time to see a haze of smoke drift upward. Virtue's shoulders had eased but he appeared preoccupied not the least bit interested in what was happening outside. He normally loved a good accident.

Finally after what seemed like an eternity the noise began to ebb until there were only shouts and the sounds of flesh and bone striking each other. In the distance the sirens of the emergency responders began to gradually build in intensity. They didn't have much time.

"Virtue, tell me what's wrong. I really need to know."

He'd been lost in thought but her question broke through his pondering. He shifted his gaze to RED and emitted a soft snort of derisiveness. "Mandy Heroic," he said between gritted teeth.

"What about her?"

He rolled his eyes and there was a brief flash of regret across his handsome features. "Mandy and I go way back. We were in flight school together. We were rivals. Veterans. Competitors..." His words trailed off and a scowl marred his forehead as his eyes became even more intense. "She died," he whispered.

Red was stunned into silence. They'd worked together for

almost twenty years ever since she had come off the assembly line at the Wright Brothers Rocket Factory. He was the only pilot she'd ever had. Until now she always considered their relationship as good friends who shared everything about their pasts. Well, at least she'd shared everything. Virtue had apparently been reluctant to share a few wrinkles from his past.

Hold on. "Who died?" she finally asked. The sirens were growing louder now. Soon the screaming fire trucks, cop cars, and ambulances would converge on the neighborhood to overwhelm their conversation.

"My girlfriend, Elsa..." His jaw locked, as the words died away his eyes overflowed with tears that spilled down his ruddy stubble covered cheeks.

Red considered the foreign sounding name for a second. "Who was she?"

"My flight instructor...and Heroic's too."

Time was fast growing short the blare of the sirens was getting closer. "Tell me."

Virtue sucked in a deep breath then let it out slowly before launching into his story. He had leaned forward in the chair his head hanging his arms resting on his thighs.

"It was just before our first solo...me, Heroic, and the five other students who hadn't washed out." The pilot academy had a high failure rate for new wanta be pilots.

Virtue continued. "Elsa had run through all our ground checks with us to ensure we fully understood the importance of checking over your aircraft before taking off. I did mine perfectly." He shrugged. "Heroic not so much. She missed a few things either intentionally or in error I don't know. Anyway Elsa was furious. She'd been pounding these procedures into us for weeks. She tore a strip off Heroic in front of us students and the ground support crew."

"I gather Mandy Heroic didn't take this well?" said RED. Virtue shook his head. "So how did Elsa die? Did Mandy seek revenge for the humiliation?" RED had just entered the land of speculation.

Virtue lifted his head to peer at RED's visual receptors. She was shocked when he shook his head again. No? I must be missing something.

"She didn't die or wasn't Mandy seeking revenge? Which is it?"

"Elsa died alright in a plane crash the next day. The official report said it was a training accident. Elsa had taken Mandy up to test her on a few things prior to her attempting the solo again. It was Mandy's last chance or she'd wash out of the academy."

Now Red was really becoming puzzled. "But I thought you said Heroic killed Elsa?"

Virtue stared at her his eyes wide. "Huh, no, Heroic didn't kill Elsa it was an accident. I just told you, the official report—"

"Oh, for God's sake, Virtue," RED interrupted the pilot, "you said you didn't like Mandy. You were angry at her."

Virtue shrugged. "I don't like her sure but she didn't kill anyone. How did you get that idea?"

"You...Elsa died...Mandy embarrassed her...." RED stopped. "Oh, forget it."

The comm unit on the desk signaled there was a call coming in ending their inane conversation. Thank you. RED opened the comm link. "Go for RED."

"Admiral Roosevelt here. We've made our decision. You and Captain Virtue have earned the right to be part of the contract. We thought your performance capturing that rogue delivery ship was excellent."

Red considered the Admiral's choice of words. Something smelled bad like rotten grapefruit. She'd never eaten grapefruit, or any fruit actually, but her aroma sensors had certainly smelled the pungent acidic fruit. It wasn't the most pleasant of odors. She could well imagine when it rotted it was really stinky.

"Why only part of the mission? I thought the contract was for the entire mission, from start to finish."

"Well we thought two teams would be better able to infiltrate the League of Evil's security and bring back the proof we need confirming the existence of their death camps."

Death camps? There wasn't anything in the submission package about death camps. She assumed the mission was a standard seek and destroy. Meaning they would get in quietly take out an ammunition stockpile or some new secret weapon then escape hopefully in one piece. But never assume is the first lesson of any mission. This was going to be very high-risk.

The LOE would do everything they could to stop the information about their death camps from getting out. Maybe Admiral Roosevelt was right. Maybe two teams were better than one. Spread the risk out a little as it were.

———

RED rechecked the sensors something she never did on a normal mission but this pincher movement with LARP and Commander Heroic to the south of the LOE command facility and her and Virtue to the north was far from the usual assault plan.

Since she and LARP both had a personal protective shielding system and could outmaneuver just about anything that flew they would hopefully survive to fly another day. The two pilots were a different matter but in the world of freelance espionage they were considered expendable. The problem she faced was Red considered Virtue a friend and as far from expendable as a human being could get. She wasn't about to cross the imaginary line to unacceptable risk if it meant something might to happen to Virtue.

She had worked closely with LARP to devise, revise, and

revise again a plan of attack until they both thought it stood the best chance of succeeding. Of course in any mission there were always unforeseen variables such as that darned human factor or human error. Humans too often had an unpredictable side of their natures that artificial intelligences had yet to crack. LARP would take the lead on the mission. No way was RED about to get into a who-has-the-biggest-rocket fight.

RED suggested they leave behind both pilots but LARP dismissed the idea without hesitation. He felt they would need the manual dexterity of a human being to rifle the files once they located them in the vast complex. His reasoning was hard to argue with so she agreed.

They attempted to pinpoint the location of the files they were after but they'd only managed to narrow it down to three possible locations. Three locations two teams. It made RED think maybe the Admiral should have hired three teams but two would have to do. It was a good thing the other team was led by LARP. He was by all reports a capable AI and very intuitive. She knew his reputation, but had never worked with him before this mission.

The weeks of preparation and planning made her a little more comfortable with him and Heroic, but in this business there were never any absolutes. It was just after midnight local time.

"Readings?" said LARP over the ghost comm. They were using a specially designed stealth communications interface manufactured by the Ford Corporation. Ford made weapons systems so why not comm systems?

"I'm showing six regiments of troopers, numerous weapons signatures including pulse rifles and seventeen air defense laser cannons." She paused to consider what a properly aimed laser canon could do to her external housing. If the housing ruptured all that would be left of them would be a cloud of radioactive dust. And everything both living and inanimate within five miles of the blast would be vaporized. She dismissed the vision of being engulfed in an atomic furnace. Her defensive shielding would protect her provided the laser wasn't a type they hadn't seen before. And since weapons development was evolving with each passing day however remote is always a possibility.

There were too many unknowns in this operation. She would have preferred six months of intelligence gathering before embarking on such a risky assault on an advanced LOE facility.

"I'm going to drop Heroic at site A," said LARP, "then proceed to site B. You and Virtue enter the complex at site C." Three red blinking lights appeared on the heads up display in Virtue's helmet after LARP transmitted the coordinates of the three entry points. RED made note of their assigned entry site on the map in her memory core.

Soon they were within fifty yards and so far there hadn't been any reaction by the defenses. "We good?" Virtue asked his whisper tense.

"So far, so good," she replied. The sensors showed the thickness of the door was ten times the other two sites. Now it made sense why LARP assigned them as a team to this location. Unfortunately they wouldn't be able to use mini-bombs to blow the door unless they used so many it would attract too much attention. Sensors indicated the lock was the most vulnerable point.

"We're coming in for a landing next to the door." RED reduced power to the thrusters as they moved to within twenty yards then cut the main thrusters and used the maneuvering jets to land them on the cement platform next to the door. The whine of the rocket motors died before they landed in a cloud of dust particles stirred up by the exhaust on the jets.

"We're shut down," RED said. Virtue acknowledged. He had his blaster in his right hand. He had set it to lethal force. She agreed with LARP they needed to apply lethal force against LOE troopers, the enemy wouldn't show mercy so why should they.

"Set your blaster on maximum, narrow beam, aim at the lock.

We need to get inside a-sap." Virtue nodded he understood. RED activated the ghost comm. "Team Two landed at site C." LARP acknowledged the signal but oddly didn't report his and Heroic's positions. Team One had deviated from the agreed upon plan.

Something didn't feel right about these anomalies but RED had no evidence to suggest the mission was compromised so she decided to proceed. She redirected some of her internal power to external sensors. Extreme caution would be her mission protocol from this point forward.

She needed to focus. "Fire," she ordered.

Virtue pressed the firing stud on his blaster and a ruby red beam of concentrated energy shot from the business end of the weapon and struck the lock. The steel composite quickly glowed yellow then red then orange. Her sensors registered the sharp increase in heat until the locking mechanism began to melt as if it were made of pudding. Virtue released the firing stud and the beam ended. He then lifted his leg and kicked in the door with his booted foot. The door swung violently inward with a loud bang. Beyond the doorway was inky blackness. There were no lights.

Caution, thought RED. "Let's go. Activate your external lights."

Virtue, the blaster pistol still held ready to fire, tapped the interface on his right brass armband covering his leather jacket and the lights on his helmet lit up. They were bright enough to illuminate an area fifty feet in circumference.

Cautiously Virtue entered the facility his boot steps echoing in the quiet. Red thought she could hear his heart beat. Her sensors detected his heart rate was up and his breathing more forced. Blood pressure and adrenaline were normal for a combat situation. He was sweating evidenced by the increase in body heat under his uniform and the helmet. Of course the presence of water molecules on his skin confirmed the other indicators.

The helmet lights lit up the corridor the right side lined with closed doors as far as the light extended. Virtue stepped up to the first of the doors. The pine door was painted steel gray and there was a plaque affixed to it that read Communications.

Without being urged Virtue moved on to the next door. The plaque read Supply. They moved to the third door and found what they were looking for. The plaque read Administration. Hopefully the records detailing the death camps would be easy to find but somehow RED doubted it would be that simple.

Virtue tried the door handle but it was not surprisingly locked. "Hold on," RED instructed and Virtue hesitated shooting the lock as he had done with the exterior door. "I'll run a full sensor scan. The door may be alarmed or booby trapped."

As she ran the detailed scans Virtue undid the chest strap of the brown leather harness holding the rocket pack in place then loosened the shoulder straps. He slipped the straps off his shoulders then set RED on the floor next to him. He took careful aim at the lock both hands gripping the pistol stock waiting for the order to fire.

RED processed the incoming sensor data and determined the door was neither alarmed nor booby-trapped. "Okay."

Virtue fired and again the brilliant red beam of concentrated energy melted the lock. After he stopped firing he tapped the door open with his booted toe of his boot. The door swung in. The room beyond was shrouded in darkness. Virtue stepped in and felt along the wall until he found the light switch. He tapped the wall plate and the lights in the room flickered to life illuminating the interior.

He stepped inside his blaster still out. After disappearing for several seconds he reappeared to grab RED by the straps and carried her into the room. He set her on one of the four large oak desks in the center of the room. They were grouped together at the center of the expansive room. The walls were lined with army green filing cabinets and inside those were two additional rows of the same filing cabinets.

This was going to take far more time than they had to sort through. "Virtue, are there labels on the cabinets?"

He shut down the external lights on his helmet then took it off placing it on the desk next to RED. He moved the closest filing cabinet. "Yes, but they are numbers. They must have a numbered filing system. And the cabinets are locked. They require keys." He hesitated unsure what to do next.

RED thought for a few minutes. She recalled a man she once knew named Dewy. He invented numbered filing system used in offices around the world. The Imperial Armed forces had even adopted the system and the military was usually the most resistant to change. Not that it made much difference but a numbered system was going to be a serious challenge without a Rosetta stone to decipher what information pertained to what number.

Her visual receptors shifted to look at Virtue when he grunted. "Say maybe one of these desks has a file list?" he suggested.

"Good idea," RED replied impressed her pilot had come up with such an obvious idea. "Start looking," she urged him.

Virtue moved to each desk and searched them opening all the drawers and rifling through the contents. There were used paper sacks that once held a workers lunch, papers with written instructions, memos from superiors, pencils, pens, metal clips for holding papers together, telephone directories and other common office materials. But nothing that looked like a file list. Finally in the last desk Virtue discovered a metal ring crowded with keys. They were small keys obviously not for doors but for the filing cabinets. But which one was for which cabinet.

We're moving like molasses on a cold day, thought RED

bitterly. Her father and creator had been right on with that saying. Winston Nemostat had been a genius in so many ways. It was at times like this she most missed his wise counsel.

How were they going to find the right cabinet? It would take far too long to check every key never mind having to review each file in each cabinet. They could get lucky however she wasn't about to depend on dumb luck.

It wouldn't be long before their intrusion would be discovered. They hadn't encountered any guards but that couldn't last. Time was growing short.

A sudden beep from the ghost comm broke through her deliberations. "Team Two."

"This is Team One. Evacuate site ASAP." The signal ended.

Had something gone wrong? Not that it mattered. They had to leave, now. "Okay, Virtue, let's wind it up. We're outta here."

Suddenly Virtue had his blaster pistol aimed at her a sardonic grin on his handsome features. His blue eyes reflected scorn. What was happening?

"What are you doing, Willie?" she said using his first name something she rarely did.

He arched one eyebrow and stepped out of range of her onboard defensive systems. The electro shock nodes and stun gas ejector tubes built into her frame could take out an enemy within a range of two feet. This prevented any non-authorized person from gaining control of her.

"I need to delay your departure," he said grimly as the grin melted from his eyes and lips.

"Why?"

When he didn't reply instead scanned the room his pistol remaining aimed at her it occurred to her he was taking orders from someone other than her. If he triggered the blaster her personal shields would hold for a few minutes at this range but once the thin beam of energy pierced the protective field her tanks would rupture. Their deaths would be quick, but she suspected that wasn't the end game at play here.

Someone wanted her and the evidence of the death camps erased simultaneously. But who?

She activated the rocket engines. The confined office space quickly filled with smoke. She lifted off the desk turned and flew directly at Virtue who was choking and disoriented. Her twin rockets slammed into his mid section causing him to emit a strangled grunt and the pistol flew from his hand. RED slammed him into a row of filing cabinets, which fell backward as if they were trees struck by hurricane force winds. Her sensors indicated his heart had a stopped upon impact with heavy steel cabinets. The office had been showered with his blood.

Knowing her pilot and close friend was dead she turned and flew to the door to the corridor. Once outside she used the sensors to find the opening to the exit. The walls and floor around her were trembling. Something very bad had happened.

Sure enough her sensors recorded a massive explosion somewhere to the north of her position centered within the facility. It occurred near the coordinates where Commander Heroic had been dropped off. The readings were heavy with deadly radiation of a type common to nuclear weapons.

RED increased the power to the rockets and her speed increased until she shot out the exit at her maximum speed. She selected a course directly opposite of the direction of spreading wave of fiery all consuming energy and shot up and away into the night sky.

The pinpoint brilliant stars dotting the heavens were still visible against the darkness but the blast wave was edging out the peripheral edges of the visible sky as it grew like a pebble dropped in a pond more rapidly than RED would have liked.

RED added every bit of internal power to the thrusters and

the speed edged slowly upward. The thrust increased beyond the design specifications. She was red lining the rocket motors. Every on board system was becoming compromised including her memory core.

Finally the motors began to shut down as they over heated and she began to tumble in the thin air. Gradually she became aware of her surroundings as her internal sensors recalibrated. She was higher in the atmosphere than she had ever been—more than 97,000 feet—and five hundred miles from where she started.

I'm gonna need a major refit.

She activated her thrusters and found her rockets were still operational having cooled enough after the wild ride she'd just taken. She started a slow spiral to reduce altitude. One the way down she thought about Virtues death and about who might be responsible for turning him against her. Who had enough influence to turn a loyal pilot against an AI and who might want her dead? She'd made any number of enemies over the years but most of them were either dead or in prison.

The League of Evil seemed an obvious suspect but they were a little too convenient. Besides destroying their own facility seemed a little drastic just to murder one AI and her pilot. But then what happened to LARP and Heroic?

She opened the ghost comm. "Team One to Team Two." Static. She tried again with the same result. Curious.

She next tried the civilian news broadcasts. After listening for several minutes she learned they were reporting a massive explosion inside LOE territory but nothing about casualties. More curious.

"RED to Admiral Roosevelt." She signaled again. This time there was a response, but on a very low frequency band. "This is a secure Imperial Security channel. Who is this?" said a curt female voice.

"This is Captain Virtue's AI, Reactive Energy Device." She

used her full name not just her code name and she transmitted the security identification code the admiral had given her at their meeting.

Whoever was at the other end didn't respond for several seconds giving RED enough time to try a long-range sensor sweep to detect any sign of LARP and Heroic but she found nothing. Not even an echo of their signal remained. This was very odd.

"Who gave you this security code?" asked the security officer in an officious and aggressive tone.

"Admiral Roosevelt."

"We have no record of an Admiral Roosevelt...in fact we have no record of you."

It suddenly dawned on RED what must have happened. It had to be the only reasonable explanation. "What year is this?" she asked.

"What does that matter?" said the woman with obvious distain.

"Please. I need to know the year."

The woman snorted through a sudden burst of static. "It's 1943. Why? I'm getting some strange readings from you lady...are you really a reactive energy device?"

I somehow must have been transported fifteen years ahead in time. RED delinked the connection without responding. The conversation was headed for planet awkward questions and she didn't want to go there.

She needed to recruit a new pilot, fast. Anything could have happened by now. It was entirely possible she might be the only AI who survived what she had to assume was a purge to remove the pilots and the AI's. The League of Evil must be behind these events.

She was not only going to fight on to rescue the empire from grip of the LOE but she would have to find a new and improved version of Captain Virtue to take the fight to whoever was responsible. Together they would be the heroes for this new age. The road ahead would be filled with danger and adventure and she was going to enjoy it.

Captain Virtue and RED will return in Captain Virtue Flies Again.

ABOUT THE AUTHORS

Rita Schulz lives on the Sunshine Coast in British Columbia with, Russ, her husband, who is also a fiction writer. She has written for many years and is an alumnus of the Oregon Writers Network, and the Greater Vancouver Chapter of the Romance Writers of America.

Her most recently published stories are Old Bones, Fire in Their Hearts with Russ Crossley, and Ladies of the Jolly Roger all published by 53rd Street Publishing.

Please visit her website at http://www.ritaschulz.com to view her other works or check out http://www.53rdstreetpublishing.com

International selling Star Trek author, Russ Crossley, writes science fiction and fantasy, and mystery/suspense as well as their various subgenres.

His latest science fiction satire set in the far future, Revenge of the Lushites, is a sequel to Attack of the Lushites released in 2011. Both titles are available in e-book and trade paperback.

He has sold several short stories that have appeared in anthologies from various publishers including; WMG Publishing, Pocket Books, 53rd Street Publishing, and St. Martins Press.

He is a member of SF Canada and is past president of the Greater Vancouver Chapter of Romance Writers of America. He is also an alumni of the Oregon Coast Professional Fiction Writers Master Class taught by award winning author/editors, Kristine Katherine Rusch and Dean Wesley Smith.

Feel free to contact him on Facebook, Twitter, or his website http//:www.russcrossley.com. He loves to hear from readers.

COLLECTIONS FROM 53RD STREET PUBLISHING

Tales of Urban Fantasy

Five Tales of Bizarre Detectives

Tales of Mystery and Suspense

Tales of Weird Fantasy

Tales of Twisted Crime

Tales of The Unexpected

Tales From Space

10 by Russ Crossley

Round Up At The Burger Bar: The Story of Trixie Pug,

Parts 1- 5 The Beginning

Worlds of Science Fiction and Fantasy

More Tales of Mystery and Suspense

Justice Served

Love Stories

Ladies of the Jolly Roger with Rita Schulz

The Adventures of Razor and Edge:

Five Tales From The Quirky Detective Team

An Unexpected Journey

On Edge

Thrilling Adventures

Thrilling Adventures 2

Total War

Courageous